In the Arms of Our Elders

In the Arms of
Our Elders

by William Henry Lewis

Carolina Wren Press
Durham, North Carolina

The publication of this book was made possible by generous grants from the National
Endowment for the Arts and the North
Carolina Arts Council. In addition, we grate-
fully acknowledge the ongoing support made
possible in part through gifts to the Durham
Arts Council's United Arts Fund.

Library of Congress Cataloguing-in-Publication
Data
Lewis, W. H. (William Henry), 1967-
In the arms of our elders / by W. H. Lewis.
p.   cm.
Contents: The days the light stays on—A man and
his son went looking for pine planks—The sun of
47 years—Moving—Leaving the dog, I saw a buz-
zard in the road—The trip back from Whidbey—
Sister got a man—Other people's houses—
Germinating.
1. Afro-Americans—Social life and customs—
Fiction.   2. Afro-American families—Fiction.
I. Title.
PS3562.E98315   1994
813'.54—dc20   94-34962
                                                        CIP
ISBN: 0-932112-35-8

Cover: "Bread, Fish, Fruit," 1985, by Jacob
Lawrence. Courtesy of the artist and
Francine Seders Gallery, Seattle, Washington.
Photo by Chris Eden.

Book and Cover Design by Hsing-Wen Chang
Art Direction by Martha Scotford

Manufactured in the United States of America

This small book has a large list of thanks. The author wishes to extend his deepest gratitude to Pop-Pop, Dennis Nathaniel Williams, Jr., James Miller, Fred Pfeil, Christopher Tilghman, and Mary Lambeth Moore.

Many thanks as well to the faculty of the University of Virginia Creative Writing Program and, of course, those wonderful souls in my MFA workshop, my second family for two years and many to come.

Special thanks to Jacob Lawrence, who kindly permitted me to grace the cover of this book with his work.

Contents

I'd like to know you whom I look at. Know, not love. Not that knowing is a greater pleasure; but that I have just found the joy of it.

Jean Toomer, *Cane*

For My Family

The Days the Light Stays On

for Nana

*O*ften there are days when the sun is too hot or the afternoons find her tired of staring at the flowers in her front yard. On days like this Lauralinda sits quietly on the sun porch, blinds drawn, and sighs to herself over a cup of hot water and lemon. There's an expression she wears, the way she holds herself, as pure and fragile as the china cup she drinks from. An image of solitude comes to mind; not one of sadness, she feels, but of calm. *Calm*, she'll whisper and not care that there's no one around to answer. She feels content, as if she has chosen this afternoon just for her.

At this late time in Lauralinda's life, there are a few constants that remain rich. California is still warm and dry, and her skin, though wrinkled gently, is still carmel-rich in tone. She still can buy the same tea at the same store down the street. Her rhododendrons are always bright, and not a single picture from her albums has peeled or been misplaced. She tells herself, out loud sometimes, the ways in which her life has remained simple. She doesn't mind reading aloud to herself the lists she makes to prove her life is not in wanting. These are the strings that hold the days together, simple and without regret.

*. . . To save pictures, dear, you don't just throw
them in some box. All of my photographs are in order. I
have never lost a one. You don't just set them aside. No,
that's not good. They yellow and crack. People's complex-
ions end up being faded out. Terrible. No, you must save
things like pictures.*

Don't use scotch tape. It yellows.

*Get an album. You should use the kind with corner
stays into which you can slide the photographs. Yes, that
kind is best, dear. Not those gaudy sorts for vacation
pictures. All of mine match . . .*

On the porch the blinds cut out the late afternoon
sun just enough so she can keep her eyes open and not
strain them. A dry haze rests between the shafts of shadow
and light, a soft, drunken warmth pouring into the room.
Maybe even a lightness to the ear, too, she thinks; no sound
in or around the porch being louder than the drone of bees
or children giggling in a sprinkler a few yards over.

On this particular day she is especially pleased
because this is the day that the Walker boy comes to help
her water and tend to the garden. He always comes on
Thursdays when the sun begins to go down. This she loves
as if he were some regular, shy suitor to consider toying
with. He is such a fine boy, the kind of child she would have
if she had children. But her idea of children, always growing
and changing, kept her from having them. If she had her way,
they would never grow too old or come to remember too
much.

But children *are* beautiful when they are very young,
she thinks, like creations of warm light, never losing the
laugh from their life. She had been a child like that. No care
or worry. Maybe like now. *Calm.* She had simple, white
dresses, ice cream in the afternoons, and two dogs to share

with her sisters and brothers. Her brothers would have been fine men, she tells herself often, but both had died early, too soon for her to place a strong attachment to the pictures she has of them. And her two sisters: they had been such dear girls, with skin rich-brown and glowing. They would have made fine daughters if their parents had lived long enough to see even the eldest reach fifteen years.

To this day, on her nightstand she keeps a picture of them as very young children. Five of them: two boys in modest wool jackets and knickers and three brilliant girls in pressed white lace dresses and shiny black shoes for their feet. It is the only picture she looks at every day.

. . . . .

Saturday is a cloudy day and Lauralinda puts on her blue rain slicker before she goes outside. She knows it will not rain, but she hardly ever gets to wear the blue one. Besides, it touches off her yellow blouse and her brown—*light* brown—skin. From the hall closet she fishes out her purse, the medium-sized black one. She smiles at its organization: a bus map in the side pocket, aspirins, scarf, extra glasses, an old non-operator's identification license, change purse, and a few Starlight mints.

. . . I've always had the lightest skin of us girls. My sister, Ella, she's always had dark skin. That makes her bitter. Oh, of course, she would never tell you that. But I can tell. The way she speaks to me. She thinks I think I'm above her because I do not look dark. She used to call me 'high colored.' I never acted any such manner. Such a nasty, jealous thing to say. She still doesn't like me. After all of these years . . .

Before she can leave, she must remember to heat the water on low so that it is ready for lemon and honey when she gets back. And her medicine. She must remember the medicine for her knees. And the list. On the kitchen table is the list for a bag of cotton balls, apple juice, a bag of lentils, some more tea, candy bars for Jeffrey Walker. She smiles, as she knows that on another day, last week maybe, she would have forgotten something. Last week she forgot her purse when she went out walking.

*. . . No **lady** goes out without her purse . . .*

As she leaves, she pulls out a mint. A small thing. Rewards like this keep her satisfied. Grasping onto her purse, she knows she is secure. Her sister would always kid her about purses.

Isn't that big ole thing real heavy? Ella would poke. But she had never been too refined anyway. She had chosen to stay in Chicago where women, not *ladies*, carried clutches.

I suppose *you* would never know how heavy a purse really is, would you, Elizabeth? Lauralinda would stab back.

Ella just laughed.

But Lauralinda knew better.

*. . . Never laugh with your mouth wide open. Don't **hoot** and howl out of control. It makes you look plain simple. You weren't raised like that . . .*

She closes the door and starts down her walk of azaleas. Halfway down the walk she stops, pleased with the simplicity and perfection of this day, and pops the mint into her mouth. She takes a step and then suddenly freezes. The porch light. She turns slowly to the porch and spits the mint back into its wrapper. It's the light. She has forgotten to turn it on. She must remember to do that; it is among the most important of all the items to remember for her midday walks. As if some instructor is monitoring her performance, she explains to herself the importance of the porch light. She believes that if she can hear it, hear herself saying it, she will remember. There is no one else to remind her.

"What if I forgot?" she whispers. The reality of knowing she might have been out and the light wouldn't be on fixes her in a slightly bent stance facing the door, but she can't move herself towards it. What if she forgot? What if she fell while she was out? What if she was mugged? What if she didn't come back before dark. What if she died . . . ?

What if she died and never came back? Everyone would know she wasn't at home. But worse, she had forgotten. The embarrassment would be too much.

She looks back at that unlit globe. When it's on, it means she still lives there. It means she is doing well. It means that she hasn't forgotten. It means Lauralinda is alive. But she stands there, not moving. She even looks up and down the street to make sure no one sees her. She tells herself that at least no one can see her standing there, looking like a strange old woman.

She knows it is simple: go turn on the light. *I'm sure Ella doesn't turn on her light,* Lauralinda thinks. She was always more responsible than Ella. And her other sister Virginia, too: *Ginny probably doesn't even bother thinking about the porch light.* But looking at it, knowing that it has been forgotten even for a moment, makes it unapproachable. The lightbulb hangs in the shadow of the porch like a dream that comes in a daze and is only felt because it has been forgotten.

She thinks of other objects that she has managed to cut out of her life, things that, if forgotten, would hurt her or make her life too complicated. A new electric stove to replace the gas one that might be left on, bars to protect windows that she'd leave open. The car. It sits in the garage unused now; she could never remember to check gas, or oil, or tires. Too much to remember.

*. . . Bright red lipstick is so gaudy. I mean it just looks cheap. Besides, how would red show up on **my** face? I'd look foolish. Dear, you must think of how you look. You've got to remember what men think of colors like that. Pale rose is much better. That color makes me feel nice . . .*

She tries to relax herself. She bends down to pull some yellowing leaves off her azaleas. She focuses on the rich magentas, the pinks, and for a moment she is consumed by the thought of how simple they are. She smiles at this.

. . . When I was younger, you had to let a man think you were shy, and so you wouldn't talk. He'd feel more confident that way. I never let it get too far, though. I'd always let on that I had a brain in me. Let's not forget, things aren't always what they appear . . .

Standing up, she looks and, yes, the light is still off. Slowly she walks to the house and slips inside. She puts the purse down, change spilling in it. She doesn't even bother to put the coins back in the pocket. She must remember to do that later. She jots that down on a note pad. Remember. Lauralinda sits down, puts the mint back into her mouth, and wonders how Ella can manage to keep herself going at her age. How can she remember everything that she's supposed to? So much to do now, so much to *remember*. So much to forget. She looks out at the pale sky and thinks about the porch light. She writes another note. She'll turn it on later.

She sits there in her blue rain slicker, sucking on her mint.
"Remember."

. . . . .

It's Thursday again. Hotter than last Thursday.
Because it is hot, Lauralinda is tired. Earlier, on her sun
porch, she had sung all the standards she knew about strife
and forgotten love. Now she smiles and laughs to herself
about the old woman that she is becoming.

*. . . Virginia never had any ambition. She should
not have been in charge. How can an older sister care for
you if she doesn't know how to care for herself? She
never wanted anything. Never left home. That wasn't good.
I've worked hard all my life.*
You have to want something for yourself. Something . . .   ——— 7

She feels that she has grown into her refinement
appropriately. She has worn the proper dresses, known the
talked-about gentlemen, gone to the in-season luncheons
and has kept a fine garden. But what is to be said for her calling up her sister in the middle of the night only to argue
about who took care of whom way back when? And what of
her sister asking her why it is so damn important to remember anyway? Her sister's son, the lawyer, keeps telling her
about the stormy existence of two entities pulling and pushing each other inside of her. But at his age, what would he
know about a woman such as she? It is now, only after so
many years passed, that she can think on this, sitting quietly
on her sun porch.

*. . . Coffee? Thank you, no. I don't care for tea, either.
I like something soothing. Water and lemon is good . . .*

She gets up from her chair and moves inside because the sun is now edging towards her toes and soon will be close to eye level. It seems to her that the glare and heat of the day is always greater on Thursdays, when she is tired. She prides herself in figuring out things like this. Some things she works on, things that are difficult to figure out or that are difficult to remember. Other things, she lets go. She moves through the living room to the bathroom looking for her cheek blush. She must find it and remember to put it on because Jeffrey Walker comes over today to help with the yard. He comes at seven-thirty, when the sun is beginning to go down and it's cooler. It is only five-thirty now, she tells herself. She has two hours.

She amuses herself with the notion that the Walker boy would have a crush on her if only she looked a bit younger. It's her little secret that she covets for entertainment's sake. And why not? She believes her skin has aged in the California sun, but the look of refinement, accented by off-white blouses or chartreuse-colored scarves, has not left. She knows that among all her relatives, her skin has always been the finest; never dark brown and ashy, but richly smooth and creamy in the manner that allowed her to be asked first to dance as she sat with the other girls along the dance hall walls. She has always felt that her appearance matched the lady she was aspiring to be.

. . . I'd never do my own grocery shopping. Too much trouble. Sheffield's down the street delivers for me. They always get my list right. And they pick the best tomatoes . . .

She takes a break from her makeup search to sit down. *Rest now, dear, be calm,* she reminds herself. On Thursdays, this is all she can do. She is tired from having

8

walked seven blocks for exercise, which she only does on Thursdays. Were it any other day, she might have more energy to stay outside and face the sunlight, or do the garden by herself, or even find her makeup without resting.

She looks for a moment at the collection of shells arranged in a basket on her hearth. She feels they haven't lost their beauty since the morning she discovered them, decades ago, hidden away in the Pacific tide pools. She must have been only twenty then, but already far away from home. It had been a morning that none of her photograph albums could have contained. With her sister, Ella, who had come to visit, and two kind young men, she had spent the whole morning on the beach. She and Ella had danced late into the night, whirling in shimmering, cream-colored dresses, their escorts in white dinner jackets. They greeted the sunrise with a bottle of champagne. She can remember Ella's complaints, too; something about there being too much water, and Black folks never went to the beach anyway.

She had wanted that time to be so ripe, so wonderful, rich enough to last through all of her bad days until the time came that she would tell it to her children as they, too, walked along some beach in an early-morning sun. Sometimes she imagines that she, like her shells, has become more beautiful with age. But there is dust on the shells. She realizes how rarely she looks at them.

On another day when she can give the thought more concentration, she might take the time to figure out why she doesn't look at them. But quickly she passes it off as something to do with all that inner-self jumble that her nephew the lawyer always bothers about.

. . . Children today are in too much of a rush. They never stop and notice anything, anybody. Just the other day, a pack of boys nearly knocked me off the sidewalk . . .

She turns her head away from the shells and closes her eyes. She remembers when sleep was not always her first response to closed eyelids. It used to be quite simply resting her mind. But she is older now. She must remain alert and it bothers her that she must remind herself to be alert. She tries to fight sleep and clear her mind so that she can find her makeup case. But eyelids never blanketed quite so comfortably as they do now.

. . . No, dear, heavens no. My hair has never been dyed. What a thing to ask. . . . Do you like it . . . ?

From way off she hears the screen door rattle.

She is startled from a fog of drowsiness. Her chest heaves, her heart pounds so fiercely that it feels as if it is on top of her.

There is a careful knock on the front door. "Miss Evans?"

She realizes that it is the Walker boy. For a moment she is shaken by her fear, having discovered herself alone, in her house, on Thursday.

"Miss Evans? You in there?"

Jeffrey Walker! But she was sure she had two more hours and her watch says . . . Her wrists are bare and she pictures the watch hanging from its gold clasp chain on the bedside lamp. She sees that the sun has now crept to just below the ceiling molding. She rises to get the door and catches half of her face in the mirror in the entry hallway. No makeup. *He'll be disappointed!* Now her mind is working. She pictures her watch and with it—no, below it on the bedside table, her makeup case.

"You all right in there, Miss Evans?"

From the bedroom door she sees the case and rushes to it, ignoring the knocking and Jeffrey Walker trying to force

The Days the Light Stays On

the screen door open. She decides that for this emergency she will only have time for base and blush, and she viciously dabs the chalky powder onto one cheek. The color is good, she tells herself, and lifts the case to check.

"Miss Evans! It's Jeff, Jeffrey Walker. I've come to do the yard. Are you all right?"

She feels angry that he should be so worried about her, as if she couldn't take care of herself.

. . . I remember when high heels were stylish, classy. Not sleazy, like now. I had twelve pairs . . .

"Miss Evans!"

She drops the makeup case. It falls and bounces behind the bedside table, an impossible reach for her. She can hear Jeffrey Walker working at opening the screen door. She feels air moving in and out of her, more moving out than in, it seems. *Why not just go and tell him it's all right?* She pauses at this but she can imagine the spectacle of her face too clearly. She gets down on her knees to reach for the makeup. Frantically, she strains and scratches for it, and she can feel the cramps surging in her arms. Rising back to her knees, she stares at the volumes of picture albums on the bottom shelf of the bedside table. The albums are neatly placed, all matching in color and aging well in the way that they should. They look like what people call "keepsakes." Lauralinda stares at her albums. The makeup case is there, behind them. She could put the albums on the bed or on the chair maybe. She begins to brush dust from one of them. There is a wrenching sound at the screen door and she thinks she can hear hinges giving way.

. . . I have my pride. Ladies should always be allowed their pride . . .

The screen door; she hears it. It's almost pried open.

She *needs* the makeup. But the albums. They're in the way. She claws at them, pulling and swiping. She clears them from the shelf with heavy sweeps of her hands. She almost could be trying to swim if there were water to drown in. She lunges for the makeup case, and her whole body settles as she feels the clammy shell. She pulls it out and makes sure she has the right side up to open it. But there is something else.

The albums. Like a child who suddenly understands the futility of breaking her own toys out of anger for her parents, Lauralinda slumps back and realizes what has become of the photograph albums. Dashed and separated, several pages and pictures litter the floor.

She lets the makeup case slide into the valley of fabric between her thighs and reaches for her favorite album. She can hear cautious footsteps in the living room, but they seem to be far away. Right now, right here in front of her, her album of family photographs has fallen apart. She rakes a pile of pictures close to her, then picks them up one at a time.

. . . *Black and whites are so much more expressive than color, don't you think? Look. Look how radiant we are in this one. And look at my skin* . . .

One after another she takes them in, realizing how much time has gone by since she last saw the people in them.

"Miss Evans? You all right?" Jeffrey Walker stands outside the bedroom door. "I thought you were hurt or something."

Lauralinda is halfway into another picture before she looks up. "Jeffrey. Hello. Child, you shouldn't worry so much." Rising slowly, she places the album and pictures on the bed.

"Sorry about your screen door."

"The what . . . ? Oh, yes. Don't worry, Jeffrey. It's all right." She can feel the strain in her throat as sound passes through it. "Have you ever looked at photos of your family, Jeff?"

Jeffrey Walker, slim, nervous, and grass-stained from the day's work, is silent.

"I think it's important to do that every once in a while. You begin to rediscover things. Things about people that have gone."

"I guess so. Look, are you all right?"

"Look at me. Dear, I'm such a pitiful hostess. We should really sit down in the living room, Jeffrey. I have something to show you." She takes one album and heads for the living room, holding the loose pictures that have fallen out. She doesn't respond to his stares at her half-done face. She sits down in a small chair, one she never sits in, but enjoys having in her home. He follows and stands in the middle of the room, looking lost.

. . . I've always liked the way I live. I don't mind. But people stare at you. They stare. Think you're crazy. They don't know how to treat a lady. The neighbors think I'm going to fall or something. Fools is what they are. They say I need family. What family? I'm not bad off . . .

She realizes how long it has been since she felt alone or completely sad. But living in a small house in California, with old pictures and dusty shells, she does ache; skin aching for touch the way glaciers ache to move. Tears, just slight moisture, come to her eyes as she hands Jeffrey the picture of a young man who used to take her in his convertible to Carmel. Jeffrey Walker crouches down in the middle of the room, unsure of the picture he cradles.

"He was so much like my brother Russell." She rises to look over his shoulders, to witness his reaction. Pleased, she stoops to find others. She sits down again, as a lady would, and the boy rises to be handed the photographs. They pass a few between them and then, like noticing a lightbulb blown out, she comes upon a certain picture.

Her body braces, jolting a high, wounded moan from her, and her eyes shut tight trying to hold it in. Jeffrey reaches and cups his hands around the space where he would support her shoulders if he felt comfortable touching her. She stiffens. Then Lauralinda Evans lurches back and laughs like she did when she was a child.

"Look at us," she says, holding the photo out. "All of us are so old now. And how tacky we all look. And look at my skin . . ." The picture: a long-gone family reunion, the fifties perhaps. Lauralinda in white, her sisters, one of their husbands, a few cousins, a crazy uncle from St. Paul, and a few other people she could name but never cared to. All of them removed now, gone; none smiling for the photographer and caught in a grip of gray.

"Crazy folks, all of them," she says. "This reunion here, 1956, it was crazy. There was so much food, chicken, ribs; I made seven pies. There was too much potato salad. These people were just plain silly. Chester with his green tie and shoes. Children everywhere. Dorice, she had the cutest little girl. I only go for the children. Some of those reunions were wonderful times, but then some people stopped coming. People die, you know. They do." She looks to Jeffrey, moisture running quickly down one side of her face and slowly channeling through the blush on the other half.

"You really miss these folks, don't you, Miss Evans?"

And Lauralinda, after pausing for a moment, rolls

back in the chair, letting out what she hopes sounds like laughter. The sound comes sharp and high-pitched, her teeth showing. It could be a wail, but she's trying to smile. It falls out, her hand not even covering her mouth, and she wonders what inside her could make such sounds.

A man and his son went looking for pine planks

*for my
grandfathers*

*. . . because pine smells
better,* he had said since years back, *got finer grain, too.*
Drinking ice tea on the back stairs, the son spread on the
lawn, he'd tell his boy how pine smelled in the woods—pine
and soil—after it rains like hammers. *The smell's got its own
way with the air and that fine soil.* The back stairs hours: that
was years ago. *Those roots, you could smell 'em, deep in the
black earth.*

Now, years from those stairs, as they stood in the
lumberyard among stacks of fallen forests, the pine was
there. *When my time come, don't want no alum'num box,*
he had said earlier that day. *Figger that: spendin' all Eter-
nity smellin' like my lunch pail. Pine, boy. Got to be pine.*
They walked along the rows, looking for the right size, color,
and the perfect match of grain. More than his eyes, the man
used his nose. *It's the smell,* he'd say. He talked down into
the moist, sawdust ground as the son followed a step
behind.

"Still seeing that gal from Fayette?" he asked his son.
But the man frowned before any answer. "No. Don't suppose
you would be, not up and away from here like you are." He
stopped, rubbed his hips, looked to the sky as if he knew

something about it. "This way," he said and headed back down a row of particleboard.

His son walked with the resolved step of a man who knew more about bargain VCRs and oat bran. And because he knew his son, the man kept an erratic pace, slowing to feel raw planks of cedar and smooth white pine, stopping to smell the air, turning his head back to the boy to let him know that he was beginning a sentence and then bolting on.

The boy, who was also a man, began to count the colors in the faded plaid of his father's work shirt. He looked at the skin, the way the dark wrinkle of his father's neck seemed to match the earth. Deep, rich, weathered, earth skin. Some folks just looked so damn dark, as if they could come from no place but the land. His aunt used to say, *some folks was just makin' ready for it.*

The father turned a sharp corner and the son stumbled to follow.

"Remember now, the grass gets mowed every Thursday and give the dogs their medicine once a month . . ." The man stopped, rubbed his head. "The truck. Make sure you turn it over every once in a while . . ." His dark neck was crevassed, as if he had crafted it under the sun his whole life.

The son stepped up to look into his father's face. It wasn't time to speak of such things. "I'll remember."

The man took off his hat. Looking into the haze of the sky, away from his son, he rubbed his neck like he could wipe the wrinkles right off. He put his hat back on and started walking. "Pine's down there."

The man was a full five or six steps ahead before the boy decided to catch up.

He looked at the father's profile, staring as if something about the surge of the cheekbone from the face was worth studying. It was the face the man could put on: a deep-set expression that pushed the cheekbones up and set the slant of his mouth into the lines that showed up when he smiled. *When* he smiled. The son figured for years now that the man practiced *not* smiling. He wore that tight-boned face so often, so hard, that its strain must have been the reason for his teeth grinding away by his fiftieth year. After that, he had taken to chewing and grinding the false teeth even when he wasn't eating. Even from slightly behind, the son could see the jaw working the fake teeth around the gums.

The man let his teeth come to a rest when he stopped. "Now it ain't just picking any pine," he said. "Got to be a good deep, tight grain. Look for dark knots and thick winter growth . . . and the *smell;* you got to be able to smell the wood." He whispered when he spoke of how it smelled. He pulled out a firm eight-inch wide plank and ran his rough hands over it, squeezed it, stuck his face right onto it. He inhaled deeply, the way a man does when he takes to noticing how he breathes. He put the plank back, pulled another, and smelled it, too. With this plank it took longer; when he pulled the board from his face and set it aside, his cheek wore the sign of the grain.

The son watched, hands in pockets.

His father reached for another. And then he pulled two more without smelling them. He pointed to the grain proudly. "Same tree . . ." he trailed off into whispering.

The son craned to listen, but he knew his father was not talking to him.

Three boards later, the man stopped and looked almost at the son, but made sure their eyes did not meet. "Your mother, she ain't all that strong anymore . . . she needs company now and then." He looked back to the wood. ". . . can't forget . . ." He drew in his breath.

"I won't."

The time passed, the son helping the man stack the pine aside, learning how to find the smell. But they didn't speak. His father would gesture, instructing with small waves of the hand, nods of the head. This had been his talk, their talk, for the past half hour, for the past half of their lives.

Not expecting surprises during such a short visit home, the son remembered shuddering when his father stretched from the breakfast table and told him where they were going that day. In the truck on the way, there was no debating: *we got to get eleven planks. Six for the sides an' bottom, two for ends. Two for the cover. One for bracing.* And riding to the lumberyard the son sat staring at the rust-out of the floor board, thinking how he had heard the same instructions-for-life voice when he first left for college. There was no hidden message. Looking for these pine planks was to be handled as calmly as birch logs to be split for winter or switching the voltage regulator in the truck. Eventually, those things needed doing. *I just want to make sure it's done proper.*

Before the son realized that the eleven planks were chosen, his father began to heft three to his shoulder and was bending for the fourth. The white pine was heavy and the years had robbed his father's body of the strength it once owned. He swayed and, like a bad stool leg, leaned and gave way.

His body had loosened under the weight instead of abruptly crashing with it, as if his frame had meant to challenge the burden and *then* collapse. The falling seemed to go slower, he thought as he lay there now, face turned to the sawdust and black soil. The wood lay across his chest, and he ran his hands over it, not to move it, but to feel its grain.

The boy awkwardly bent toward his father, as if his outstretched arms would help. His feet quickly, unwillingly becoming rooted. He just stood there, his arms not quite touching his father.

A Man and His Son

With his face turned to the side, the man focused in on the world at an angle. He lay still, knowing that after this, his back would never be his own. He exhaled slowly. He couldn't see his son, but so closely attuned to the ground, he could *feel* him, stretching out, not really to help, but straining, reaching. He could feel the presence of his son, who was also a man, being rooted right there. The father smiled and thought how easy it would be to move very freely, loosely, his soles brushing grass tips. *And so soon . . .*

Even with his face halfway in the dirt, he could see down the row of stacked lumber. Wood and soil all around his body. He could hear his son breathing.

And quietly, softly, as if he had never spoken before, he whispered, "The wood . . . it smells *so* fine. So fine in the earth . . . "

The son nodded, but felt like someone who is surprised by a large owl hurtling through the forest. For a moment it was that same shock, being startled by life right there in his face, and the chill of loneliness in the middle of the dark. Then he felt his foot move and his body bend slightly. A new rush of purpose made him want to touch his father.

The man, greeting pain, turned to meet his son. The father's face was calm, and he pushed off the planks that rocked across his body.

The son reached down to help, but the man raised his hands, palms up. They looked at each other, and the boy thought he could feel roots in his feet again.

He made a second attempt to take hold of his father and again the man stopped his son with his palms. And as the son rose up away from his father, it seemed as if the expression on the old man's face was saying *not quite yet; just a little longer.*

The message seemed clearer, and yet the son realized that he had known it before. The sight of his father resting in the soil allowed him the vision of what might happen in days to follow. He only knew of the inevitable need situations like this would present to him at random times. Like the tricky voltage regulator in the truck. There was no reason to it. All a soul could do was make ready.

And now he imagined the ride back in the truck: his father, sitting very still, elbow out the passenger window, not saying a word. For even though the father might smile, even though the son might see a new look in his father's face, the father had never *not* driven the truck.

The father also felt the weight of the ride to come. He would watch the countryside roll by him on his way home. He would be proud, his son handling the muddy roads well. Even above the throbbing in his back, he would be more aware of the air moving in his chest. He would see the green of the trees again. He would notice the deepness of the forest, radiant yellowing birch trees and great tulip poplars, far off, edging the fields. At this, he might smile.

The father could hear someone coming now, feet pounding on the earth. He looked at his son and pointed to the wood planks.

His son looked back at him, at his father's hand. The palm was still raised and smeared with soil, but rich and blackish-brown as if it had been painted there.

A Man and His Son

The Sun of
47 Years

for my mother, her mother,
and mothers who
don't know their own

*F*rom where I lie I can hear the early call of larks in the trees outside. The stillness of my bedroom. I think of this when I hear them. It's 6:30 in the morning and I'm in bed, with Steward, but it's cold. My eyes aren't even closed. A pain in my body, my hip or back, maybe my head, has kept me like this for the past hour. I would like to see the deep-red shades slipping down the insides of my eyelids, not the gray of the ceiling at 6:30. But Stephen needs to get up for school, and Nick will be coming home in two days. And, of course, there's Steward. After twenty-five years, he still needs me to find the coffee for him in the morning.

I know how lonely I will feel at the table on Thursday with my children and my husband next to me. Thanksgiving dinner. We will be holding hands, praying for the food on the table, but I will feel cold. I won't taste the dinner that I made, or notice the flatware that Steward's parents gave us. I won't see the hair that hangs in my eyes because I didn't give a damn about combing it before supper. I will be thinking of something else, like this gray ceiling.

I must get up now. The dog is scratching at the back door, and Stephen will forget to feed him before he goes to school. I must be up to feed Stephen and make him drink all his milk, to give Steward his vitamins and coffee, to make sure the dog gets fed, prepare to have my eldest son home.

The thought of a shower makes me feel good, but then there's Chester, silly old dog. I can hear him playing with his bowl on the porch. I rub my thighs to warm them, get up, and walk towards the kitchen through the back hallway. The sun isn't here yet. I feel along the hallway, listening to the brush of my slippers on the carpet. My hand, as if it has not become fully conscious, slides along the wall. It feels the cracks and chipped paint that have needed attention for years. I stop near the bathroom. A few feet from the door, lower down on the wall, there's a familiar spot. A lump, a small bulge under the wallpaper. My fingers massage and move the bits of wall plaster that have settled there. They crumble and rustle against each other. There is nothing special about this part of the hall except that I know it well with my hands. I know it well because I feel for it every morning. I feel it every morning when the sun has not risen yet to light up this house.

I take the flannel robe from the hook on the bathroom door and go to the kitchen. The shoulders of the robe feel soft on my skin and remind me of my mother when I would go into her kitchen on cold mornings and watch her, in the red robe, making me hominy and bacon. I smile to myself as I count the holes around the undone hem at the bottom of the robe. I call it my feeding dress.

In the kitchen I go straight to the stove, turn on the oven, and open its door. The radiator hasn't worked in the kitchen for years, but the stove has always been my warm companion in the morning. I'm reaching for my tea bags when I hear large paws scratching on the back screen door. Chester is waiting. I open the door and cold takes my body.

I need to have more on and I breathe heavily, feeling the shock of an early-gone autumn. Through the steam of my breath I see the silhouettes of birds moving through the trees. I open the back door wider and Chester shoves a paw through one of the holes in the screen door, waiting for me to open it. I pat his paw and push it back through. He lets me open the screen and tries to sit patiently, but his tail can't help its eagerness. I bend down to pick up the bowl. The cold air sinks into me.

Standing up, I see it. Through the naked beech trees and across the valley, I see the gray of the hills warming to orange from the first touch of sun. The sight warms me, even though it's still too low to do me any good yet. Two mornings from now: that's when Nick's plane will be coming from where the sun crests the hills.

The sun has brightened the sky a little, enough to make out layers of soft yellows along the ridges of the valley. It looks so warm out there, but I'm still shivering. It is on mornings like these that I think about my mother. She is tired, too.

Sitting next to a table covered with old magazines and half-filled milk cartons, I wait. I clear the table so I can put my package down. The sun is warm at this section of the airport concourse. I got here early just to sit facing the large windows, feel the sun, and watch the plane lower over the hills. I want to see it first. My eyes are tired and the glare is strong, so I turn back to face the rest of the people in the room. I notice a woman right across from me, flipping through a magazine.

"Hello, Judy."

She stirs, puts down the magazine, and nods. She curves her lips politely, but it seems like an effort. Judy Waters didn't look like this last week when I saw her at church. She seemed content, smiling then, not holding herself so tightly like she is now. She was deep in prayer. I wondered why she looked so comfortable. Then I realized that she was sitting alone. Her family would be tucked in bed at home, their brunch warming on the stove and her at 8:30 Service, alone and praying.

"What's the gift?" Judy says.

"What?" I had forgotten the box beside me.

"Your package." She has put down the magazine and she leans forward, interested. She hugs her arms tightly to her body.

"Oh, this. It's for my son."

She nods and hugs herself again, as if it is cold, but I think she wishes she had something to give her son. How much we might be alike if we were both sitting there alone and hands empty, waiting to hold nothing more than our sons. But I have a sweater; this helps me. She looks at my hands as they smooth over the surface of the box, then lifts her head. For a moment we stare at each other. Because of the sun behind her, it is hard to see if the curve in her cheeks is frowning or smiling. She must be wondering why I'm holding my box so tightly. But then she looks down at her magazine again.

"It's a sweater," I say.

She nods.

"It's green."

"You must be excited to see your son. It seems like you've got things ready."

"Yes, I've been working on it. We'll all have a great big dinner, get fat on dessert, and visit some friends. I think it'll be a good time."

She says nothing.

"What are you planning to do with your son?"

"Not much. Just sitting at home, talking. We might rent some movies. Just take it easy."

But I've been through that sort of vacation before. I know what will happen. They will get home, he'll put his bags in his room, go to the T.V., and be on the couch the whole time. And she will sit in her dining room or study, wondering how long it will be before they have their first fight. I smile and say, "That sounds good, Judy."

Are you planning anything special?" she asks.

"Oh, you know . . . ," all I can do is smile, ". . . lots of things."

"I'm sure you'll have a great time. That dinner sounds like quite a show." A plane is announced over the loudspeaker. Judy gathers her magazine and coat together.

"I'm sure we'll do some shopping or something. You know, something fun . . ."

"That's nice." She rises. "I hope it's a good visit for him. I'm sure you've missed him a great deal." She gives a small wave and walks over to the gate where her son must be arriving.

I *have* missed Nick. I've got to remember to tell him that. I look around and wonder how many people here are waiting for their children to come home. How many of them are *wanting* their children to come home?

I'm convinced that Nick needs to be close to home. I know now, as I wait here alone, that he should have never left. Massachusetts is so far; it's always far. And Atlanta is too much out of mind, too damn far from Massachusetts; too easily forgotten and hard to come back to. He left so quickly, deciding on his own to go to school up North. And I told myself that I let him go willingly.

From the edge of the sun, the gleam of wings brings my son home. By the time I get to the gate, passengers are filing off. Then I see him. He is so tall. His hair is different. I keep telling myself he is older now; he is his own person. So grown. But I still see pictures. Pictures of an ashy-elbowed boy on a lake, messy hair and holes in his back pockets, worn from the skipping rocks he carried.

"Hello, Mom." His voice sounds so much better than it does on the calls from hundreds of miles away. I grab him and I try to hug him harder than he holds me. I put all my feelings into my arms until they are tingling and Nick is stiffening. And somewhere, inside of me, escaping a mother's sense of reason, I won't let go. It feels so good to touch him, to feel him *here:* home. And I cry. For a moment I push myself into believing that these tears will convince my son never to leave me.

Nick breaks free of my grasp and I realize that a boy his age would rather not be embarrassed like that.

"Sorry," I whisper, smiling at him, and we walk to the baggage claim. I'll be happy. Holding his arm is enough for now. We are leaving just as I remember my package. I tug him over to the table, reach down, and hand the package to him. He mock-sniffs the wrapping paper and gives me a knowing smile.

"Thanks. And it's not even Christmas."

He hands it back to me and puts his coat on. I am not disappointed. There's no way he could possibly open the package and put on his coat at the same time, I tell myself. Be happy that he is home.

"It's okay, Nick, you can open this later." I grasp his arm.

By the time we get his bags and head to the outer doors, I think he has grown tired of me saying how glad I am to have him home. I'm still holding the package when we get outside. *He'll open it later.* As we leave, I see Judy Waters and her son waiting for a taxi. He is a large young man and she can only reach around to his shoulder blades. They're sitting down. She has no gift to give, but they are holding each other tightly, rocking just a little. She is smiling and she holds her son as if he were a child, as if her small arms could still pick him up and rock him for hours.

. . . . .

My mother called from the hospital tonight. The phone in the den woke me from the couch at 10:30. She called at that time because it was still early, she said. She didn't want to interrupt supper. Mother always forgets that what may be 7:30 to her in Sacramento is 10:30 here. But I didn't tell her the difference of the time zones tonight. I've told her before, knowing she runs on the daily cycle of T.V. She is too tired, too worn with age and forgetfulness to put her energy into anything else. She gets up when the Service begins on the morning prayer channel, she has physical therapy when Joan Rivers is over, she eats lunch during the noon news, and she calls me once a week when the 7:00 movie is on. I remind myself not to get angry at her when she calls. It would only get her excited.

She didn't talk long tonight. She never does. I have decided that she calls every Wednesday to show me that she's not losing touch. And to show *herself* that she hasn't lost it yet, that she can still get up from the T.V., still dial the phone, still remember that she loves her daughter. She calls to tell me something new every time. It's nothing that's ever pressing or very long, but just something she feels she must tell someone before it's too late: details about my childhood, stories of the way we've grown.

They are always things that are special, things that I can tell are precious to my mother by the way her voice quivers when she recalls them. They are memories my mother deprived me of when I was young, things that she has waited thirty years to say. Or perhaps they are things that she just couldn't say until now.

And I try hard to just listen. So much of it I hear for the first time, and I know it's important to her for someone to listen. Sometimes I find myself almost pressing the receiver down out of anger or pain. I ache because I realize the hurt that she has been through, that she is going through. I know the hurt she has suffered is the pain that I suffer from now. And sometimes, in the middle of sentences, she drops off into silence, but I can hear her weeping and the T.V. turned up to drown it all out. It's so silent and clear on the phone. And lonely. So much so that my mother's quiet weeping is loud enough to make me imagine how alike we may be. I realize what I have become now and what I will be like when I get older. . . . *When I get older.*

She hung up not too long ago, her nurses always cut our talks short when she gets tired, but I still hear her voice. Tonight she didn't tell me any stories or memories; she told me how much she loved me. She said she missed the girl that was me thirty years ago, the girl she never told things to thirty years ago. I close my eyes. Tears are pushed out. I can see the same wetness rolling over the creases and coarseness of my mother's cheeks. I open my eyes and lower my head. The phone receiver still hangs from my hand.

The light has dimmed and the room feels closer now. Someone is standing in the doorway, blocking the light from the living room. It's Steward. His shadow stretches thinly across the room. It is my husband.

"Been on the phone a while."

"Yes, yes I guess I was."

"It's almost eleven o'clock."

I hang up the phone and look at him.

"I'm sorry, Steward."

"Me and the boys . . . We were just wondering . . .

We didn't quite know when you wanted to take the casserole out of the oven."

Outside, leaves pushed by a strong wind bounce off the screen and I think how cold it is.

"I'll be right there. Just a minute." My voice comes out a little weaker than I would like Steward to hear. He takes a step in the room, and I look up at him. He stops and leans towards me, hands massaging thighs inside his pockets.

"You don't *have* to come. I just wanted to know when to set supper out. It's getting late and the boys are—"

"Dammit, Steward, I said I'll be right there."

"Look, all I wanted to know was when to put the supper out. It's been in there a while. Hell, it's probably burned now. I just wanted your help."

I feel calmer now. "Sure, Steward, I'll be right there . . . ," I look up at him, "to *help* you."

Then he looks at me. I haven't wiped my eyes yet. He scratches the back of his head and looks out the window.

"Is something . . . wrong?"

"Nothing. Just nothing. I'll be right in. Tell the boys to wash up."

"They already have a while ago. Are you all right? What's wrong?"

I stare at the phone. "Steward, just go in the kitchen and sit down! I don't feel well, okay? I'm tired. And I'm *sorry*. I'm sorry! I'm sorry about the dinner and it being late, and yes, dammit, it probably *is* burned! I'm sorry! I'll get some money so you can take Nick and Stephen to goddamn McDonald's. And I . . . ," I pick up the phone and set it in my lap. "Mother called today—from the hospital. She is much worse, very sick. She is . . . tired."

He stuffs his hand back in his pocket, shifts his feet. His mouth is open, but he's silent.

I keep staring at him. "I'll be right there."

He turns to leave the room. He stops, turns his head towards me, "I'm sorry." But his voice fades into the space of the living room as he walks through it.

I listen to dry leaves brush past the window outside and wonder just what he is sorry for. I massage my face, working tears into my skin, and I remember my mother's voice, the tired tone of it, and the breathlessness it tried to hide over the phone.

· · · · ·

There are some nights, like tonight, when I think of my family, my mother, me, and I begin to question the warmth I don't feel anymore. There have been nights when I've been awake in the early dark of morning, lost in a numbness that I wasn't familiar with. I've come to know it now. It's an absence of what I used to feel: warmth coming from Steward, my sons, this house. On nights like tonight, hours after my mother has called, I remember strained images and hard years that have passed. I remember a girl in high school. Or was it college? Was she even a girl? The confusion comes from trying to figure out just when I had to stop being a girl and what made me have to become someone who had trouble calling herself a woman. On many cold November nights I have used the excuse of marriage. But I know better than that now. My mother once told me how easy it was to fall in and out of love when you're married. I wonder if she knew how hard it is to fall out of marriage. Or did my mother not run out of love before my father died?

When I feel lonely late at night, when I can't sleep, I go to the guest room. I tell myself that I will sleep there, but that doesn't happen much. Instead, I go to the guest room closet and reach beneath the quilts for a box of pictures, the pictures I see on dark mornings when I hear birds, or when I think of my children, or when I hear my mother's stories.

I separate them; old from new, color from black and white, glossy from worn. Often I look at them, hoping that the images will clear up my confusion, but the color in them fades and blurs together. They become hazy and they begin to seem the same. The black and whites become just as vivid as the color. Does the one of a knock-kneed girl in a bright white dress at the '51 Kansas State Fair seem any different from the faded image of her in a red Christmas coat years later? More and more I realize that they all tell me the same thing: how lost I feel *now*.

Many hours after my mother has called, I find myself on the guest room closet floor, allowing the pictures to hurt me. And each time I'm trying to figure out why, always a little deeper into it, always feeling more lost. There are no clear, easy ways to choose your sadness. It's a pitiful exercise: *last night was my bad night, today I will feel happy, tomorrow I will love everything, everything.* Then comes the next day. Next week. Another year. Again I find myself sitting in the dark, on the closet floor, trying to recognize memories in pictures with a flashlight. I laugh at myself, laughing and crying.

Usually I hear myself and I stop. I get silent. I stop sometimes so my youngest son down the hall won't hear me or so Steward won't wake up and find himself alone in bed. And tonight, Nick is home, so I must not wake him either. I mean, what would they do, each of them feeling cornered in their rooms, listening to sounds that they can't distinguish as laughter or crying?

Tonight I catch myself and the laughter stays inside. I silently look through the photos. I'm enjoying myself. Sometimes some of the old, worn black and whites make me smile. I can't even distinguish the figure of my father, in his Sunday suit, from the house behind him. It is one of my favorites. Years and carelessness have made the distinct black and white drift into gray.

I remember the story behind the poorly focused picture of two smiling newlyweds. My father once told me how he first asked my mother to dance when Ella Fitzgerald swung the place at The Del Ray Club over on Calvert Street. He asked her only because he was the only one of his friends not dancing, and she was there. How wonderful she looked that night, sitting in a row of empty chairs. She looked so invitingly separated from everyone else. Not pretty. Just alone. She didn't even have a nice two-tone iridescent cocktail dress like the other girls. And when he was holding this girl, he knew he would bring her there again. In a new dress. She'd never sit against that wall again.

I remember my father's teeth as he smiled and talked about those days. I close my eyes and see my mother trying to pretend that she couldn't dance. Calvert Street was good then. I hum a song that I remember my mother playing over and over one day. Ella Fitzgerald will make you do that, she told me. Tonight I want to wander through songs, never completing one, and forget how time passes.

Suddenly I hear a sniffle at the door. I stop humming. I look up and see Stephen, staring at me with little eyes that aren't used to being up this late.

"Mommy, why're you singing now?"

I smile. Smiling is important now. He doesn't need my confusion to keep him awake, too. Or my singing. I can't expect him to know what "Mood Indigo" is all about. How strange I must look, humming on the floor of the closet, shining a flashlight from a box of pictures to the jungle animals of Stephen's pajamas. But I smile because he doesn't understand. Seeing him in the ray of the flashlight, I wonder if I will tell him the important things that he should know. *Both*

34

of us don't understand. Then I think about the stories that I will keep from him until he is gone and away from me. I wonder how many kids my children will have—how many years will go by—before I decide to tell them about the pain that they felt, but couldn't explain to themselves. I think about how long it will take me to feel as if it is almost too late to tell anyone.

I look at Stephen, leaning there against the door, too young to realize what I can't explain. I see my youngest child getting older and older right in front of me and I realize how Nick has already aged, matured too soon, in a New England that he knows is conveniently distant. I think of Steward down the hall never waking up to know that I'm sleeping in the guest room. And I think of me here, in this house. I can't even remember where it was that I once smiled when some woman said something about it being too cold, too empty, for her to live in her house anymore with her children gone and husband dead. I had smiled then. It sounded like a good excuse. What's mine?

I think of this house, of this family. And my mother and me. When was it that I stopped pointing out to her ways that she was denying herself the life she deserved? I must have been somewhere in my house, lost in the kitchen or basement or ruffling through a dusty box of pictures, searching for the parts of me that I had denied or forgotten. This much becomes clear tonight: I remember feeling cheated and mocked, like I could hear my mother laughing at me for what a fool woman I'd been, lost among the men and dust of this house, all of my important parts stolen or withered. I realize I've never liked the way my mother laughed at me, kidding me about how, before I knew it, I'd be just like her.

. . . . .

The car's heater has taken several minutes' driving time before it begins to warm Nick and me. I've got my mother's red flannel robe folded on my lap. I brush it with my hands so the nap lies in a deeper shade of faded red. My fingers move quickly, stiffened by cold, but anxious to be useful. Nick took too long getting up and loading my big suitcase into the car. I shouldn't be nervous; we'll make it to the plane on time, but I can't stop my hands from squeezing Nick's arm. He hasn't said a word. I know he is tired and probably angry, too. Because he is angry and because he is trying to act like a man-of-nineteen, he has not spoken yet. He is trying to show me that he has a tolerance for things that he can't understand, but frustrate him anyway. I wonder if his frustration will get in the way when he must tell his father where I have gone. That's hard for him, and I must remember not to kid him about how he might grow to miss his home. I consider him now: coming home—when he really didn't want to—to see his family, but being there only long enough to see his mother leaving.

I can see him thinking, I can hear the thoughts running through his head: *What the hell is wrong with her?* Sitting here, watching my breath become mist in the car, I know that this is hard for him. It has been that way for so long. It's hard for him to figure out his confusing mother when he's gone, but at least he's *away,* far from home. I know that is what he must think when I hear his impatient voice on the phone, anxiously trying to end the conversation. It must have been the same for him this morning when I woke him up and told him to take me to the airport. I stood outside his door for twenty minutes before I decided to wake him. When I finally did it, he just sat there in the bed. A child's eyes asking *why?* A bitter mouth saying nothing.

Even as I sat in the car waiting, I wondered why I was doing this to him. I look at him now, trying to show me how concentrated he is on the road. I turn to look at the steam rising from the river we are crossing, and I try to remember why Nick told me he wanted to go away. Or was it that he couldn't tell me?

All of this must make Nick sure of why he has gone to college up North. Being too close to home would mean being too close to a woman he must consider crazy. What is wrong with her, he's thinking. I'm leaving his father, escaping the family, he must think. Perhaps I am leaving them all, trying to get away from the dark weight in that house. But there's more. My mother.

A pain inside of me knows that I won't explain to him what he is feeling until he is much older. Until he is old enough to be silent in front of his wife when she sits at the breakfast table with him, watching him read the paper instead of eating the food that she has risen early to prepare. When he gets that old, he will begin to think back to what he feels now. And then, when he is mad, disillusioned, or angry, or lonely, I will feel it and I will call him on late nights and explain to him why he has feelings that keep him awake in the dark. And he might get angry with me, hang up on me, or he might become more confused. Maybe he will not know what to say as he hears me trying not to cry on the phone. Perhaps he will hear me trying to tell him *I'm sorry* in the way that I tell him stories of his childhood.

Maybe then, when he has grown old enough, he will come to me. I will put my weight on him and he will comfort me. Both of my children will. Maybe they will drop what they are doing, drop their depression and the deprived parts of themselves, forgetting how I made them, and travel back to me. Maybe they will come a great distance. Perhaps it will be land crossed by plane, like now, or maybe they will travel the space between us in a room. They will come to me and make me feel as if everything really was all right, as if they really hadn't grown up to be like me. They will be older and they will come to tell me that they love me when I have forgotten that they have.

I love my mother. I squeeze the folded red robe in my lap and I know that I do. I feel the time is so close now. I don't want to be too late. I think now that my mother wanted me to be there for her, to get there in time. She didn't say goodbye for the last time when I talked to her yesterday. She didn't want to, not yet. She is waiting, I have decided. As I think back, I realize how her voice was changing every Wednesday night, how every Wednesday she was trying to tell me she was sorry. And every time she called, I didn't realize it was getting nearer. I didn't realize she was waiting. She needs to wait just a little longer: to see me, to see that girl of thirty years ago, to remember that she still loves that girl. The confusion that I feel is different now. It makes me wonder why I only smiled at Stephen last night, never answering him, and it makes me try to figure out why I will never bring myself to tell my husband why I sleep in the guest room. It makes me wonder why I hold this red robe in my lap, bringing it to a woman, dying alone and tired, far away from me. I must care for her. But it will take the whole plane trip and maybe longer to figure out why I have waited until now.

"Nick, you *do* understand, don't you?" I touch his cheek, his skin so tight. "It's just that I . . ."

"Sure, Mom," he says, looking at the road, "I understand."

I see the airport far off. I try to hear in my head how my voice will sound when I tell my mother that *I* understand. When is it that anyone is ready to lie to a dying mother?

I reach into my coat pocket and take it out. The picture. Nick turns his head for a moment as he feels my hand relieve his arm. The picture: a blur of gray. A grayness that bonds a mother and a girl, sitting on a strip of Sacramento lawn, smiling only enough to please the photographer. The gray makes the two of them seem to fall in and out of the memory almost as a single thought. The faded blue ink in the corner shows a date that labels a time I can't remember clearly. I see them there, together. The same.

I feel like throwing the picture out the window, but I don't. I keep it. I breathe. I remember. I suppose that is why pictures are taken. It is all I see now and I can't help but see others. I see my father taking the picture. I see my mother waiting for him to hurry up. And I see all the other pictures, even the ones not taken yet. I see the one of Steward, realizing I'm gone, realizing I've left him, realizing that it doesn't bother him, not yet. He's sitting at the kitchen table, wondering where I keep the coffee. I see Nick, a frustrated boy. He is in a small room in Massachusetts, thinking he is better off because he doesn't have to deal with me and things like taking me to the airport on the same Thanksgiving weekend that I begged him to come home. And little Steven, forever a child, tired and confused in the middle of the night. As I'm looking ahead I see another picture: a family, all in the same frame, but standing as far apart as they possibly can.

Pictures: the kind that I will not want to put into the box in the closet. For a moment I ache, wanting the darkness of the guest room in my house.

Then I see the picture of me with my dying mother, the dead life in her, life dying in me. I see the picture already graying. The grayness becomes both of us. I see myself being with my mother, being just like my mother. The same. I think I hear laughing. Before I can tell if it's coming from my throat, before I can tell if it's even in the car, I scream. I feel my throat, the cold at the tips of my fingers, the tightness of my face as sound spills out of it. I can imagine my face, by body crouched into this car seat. My hands brace against the dashboard, and I'm feeling my mother's weight. I'm thinking *this is what mother must be like, this is what I'm going to,* and I can't stop screaming.

Nick is startled, although he doesn't want me to notice that. But I can feel the way he's stiffened. He feels my hands tugging at his shirt, sweat onto cotton, nails into his arm. He jerks his head towards me and keeps the car steady. My throat will allow no more sound and I drift into a stillness. My hands let go of the dash. And my mother is waiting for me.

"Nicholas, turn the car around."

He lets his foot off the gas, and I brace myself. He pulls the car off the road.

I'm looking straight ahead, but I know what his face must look like.

"Just turn back, Nick. Let's go home."

"What—what are you saying? Why . . . ?"

"I don't want to go now, Nick. Not now." I look at him. He is still trying to figure out what he wants to ask. His hands grip the wheel tightly, and I know how he must feel as I watch the skin stretch across his knuckles.

"Mom, I don't get it . . ." A car speeds past, blaring its horn at how poorly we are half-pulled off the road. I don't think Nick even notices it. I stare at the angry set of red taillights driving towards the airport. Nick stares at me.

"First I fly home to see the family for a nice—no, I came here for *you*! You said, 'please.' All for a *good family weekend.* And then you tell me you're leaving, getting the hell out! I didn't get it, but I did what you wanted; I'm driving you now, doing just what you said—anything for *you,* Mom!"

As he yells, I almost smile. I understand it. He will not. "Nick, I think we should talk later. I know this is hard, but I need to think now." I think he is startled at how steady my voice sounds: calm, quiet.

He leans his head back on the seat and huffs out misty breath. "Mom, I just want to understand." In the strain of his voice I hear a boy that I used to hold too tightly and love too carefully. "I just wish you would tell me why. Tell me what's going on."

"I've just rethought what I'm doing." I touch my face. I feel the change in the air that tells you when night has ended. The lights of the trucks at the airport down the road glitter in a mixture of fog and worn night.

"What if you don't ever get to see Grandmom . . . ?" he says, his tone unsure. "What if she dies?"

I can almost guess when the sun might rise.

"Nick, I know what is going to happen now. I shouldn't be there for that. I think . . . She'll be fine without me right now. It's best."

Without looking at him, I know he still doesn't understand. It will take a while. I rub my eyes and hope that the next thirty years will not be too hard for Nick. Maybe it won't take that long. He might realize before long why old people tell stories and why sometimes aging people don't like to look at pictures that tell them what they will turn out to become.

The airport, as I look at it one more time, is set in haze that reflects the beginning of sunrise. I look at my hands and realize that they are gripping each other tightly, pressing down on the picture and the faded fabric of my mother's red robe. I pick up the picture and try to focus on it. Grayness. But now, I know. *I know.* I can even handle her laughter that I imagine. I put the picture down on the seat. I lean my head against the door and watch the crescents of mist my breath makes on the window. I close my eyes and hug myself for a long time, so long that I'm not sure when I will be ready to loosen my arms. I think of my husband, my children, the cold that will come in January, the mist of the trees in the morning. And I think of my mother. And me. I think of how silently I will make breakfast in my mother's flannel robe this morning. Then, when everyone has left the house for the day, I will walk to the back hallway of the house, sit down, and feel the crumbled plaster in the bulge of old wallpaper.

Moving

for Leslye

*T*HEM
   The hallway was a lesson in simplicity: a battered brass umbrella stand with no umbrellas in it, a small ceramic tile-topped mail table, a classically frayed rug and dried flowers in a large urn. And then there was the bannister. It came flowing down from the second floor to greet all guests with its worn, cherry-wood innocence. If the sales agent could have read what the Stills were so busily scribbling in their notebooks, she might have read descriptions such as these.

   It was their insulated view of life and the objects anchoring it that were often the core of Helen and Willie Stills' dialogue. There had been gestures of love such as the Chippendale wing chairs he bought last year. She had already considered their final resting place before they had even walked into that house on Morningside Circle. The room with the bay window was begging for those chairs. And what of the teal-colored porcelain vases they bought outside of San Francisco? Those, of course, would end up garnished with dried greenery on the mantelpiece. But it was the front hallway that sold them. They were shocked that it could present itself so humbly and yet not be improved upon. Only something as unobtrusive as a bannister would stir souls like theirs.

There was a specter of appropriateness to the place on Morningside Circle. The foyer was profound and dim, dressed in light cherrywood-panelled walls, the stairs leading up into a deeper wood-stained darkness. That was not to be ignored, they felt. Actually, he would tell you it was just her. The bannister had gotten into *her*. How ridiculous, Willie Stills thought, a bannister showing itself off. And yes, the notebooks were her idea too. Steno pads. Helen Stills was one of those that reveled in the spectacle of things: shoes organized in a closet in just the right manner, the shade of cobalt blue instead of faded indigo in a bathroom, or shopping at the farmers market because the fruit looked fresher when it still had dirt on it. These were the visions that had shaped her life. If this new house's foyer had been a lesson in simplicity, the Stills' old home was a masterwork in precision without complexity.

It had been her idea all along, he felt. He really didn't know much about it at all, this business of putting pillows in just the right spot of a window seat or choosing the right type of fern for a pantry. A *pantry*. Where you keep canned goods and the dog sleeps. It didn't add up to much for him. In college he took interior design and art history *pass/fail*. Or was the grade designation for him really *care/don't care*? He had been a good guitar player and was the star of intramural soccer. He *didn't* care.

So when the day came that she said they must move to get on to a better place in life, he didn't ask her to explain if their moving was meant to be a physical action, mental transition or a fashion statement. He just said *okay*. He wasn't given to the ways of noticing detail or understanding the need for creating environment. He didn't have to be; he just adapted. She did it all and he really couldn't complain. He wasn't given much to complaining, either. But then again, Willie Stills wasn't given much to anything.

HER

Well, Mother, I've told you before; we're *not* in any financial trouble. We just—what'd you say?

No. No, Mother! We don't need any money.

Mom, we're just fine.

What?

Well I—dammit! I'm sorry, but it's the cord on this phone. It's all tangly and I can't get into the boxes and—

Mom, I don't care if 'tangly's' not a word. I'm trying to move in here. You're as bad as Willie sometimes.

No. Look, I'm sorry.

I really should go.

Yes, Willie's just fine. I've sent him on some errands. Plants, baskets, ah, lamps . . .

No, I don't need towels. I've already picked them out. Mother, you should see the bathroom!

No, Mother, *I* picked them out. He wouldn't know if they were towels or military gauze! Willie was reading the paper or watching a game or something. You know how he is.

Don't say that. I'm fine.

Look, I've got enough on my mind. This move has helped already. I'm so glad to be out of that dreary house. I don't think we ever really had fun there.

Yes, Mother, we're talking to each other. We're fine. We're *fine*.

What?

I'm serious. I can't hear you that well. This phone . . .

No, we haven't gone out yet. The house has to be taken care of. Can't just leave it and expect it to get done. Who's going to move us in?

Get serious, Mother. You know him.

No, Mom, it's all right.

We're *fine*, Mother, stop asking me how I am. I'm not sick or anything.

Mother! We're fine.

THEM

Many of the homes along Morningside had the appearance of being adorable to live in. But the Stills, claiming to be *post*-yuppie, considered themselves in the higher echelon of home-hunters in which the "internal aura" of the living space was more essential. Anyone could carefully choose the right shades of trim to paint the rain gutters or let a sun deck age into that subtle lure of brownish-gray, Sunday-afternoon perfection. But it was the inside that told whether or not a house was truly livable. Houses had ways of being deceptive with their perfectly arranged oversized coffee-table books and green marble mantle pieces. The Stills had seen it all. After all, they had had art history and interior design as electives in college. And those were *good* colleges. And the Stills *were* post-yuppie.

HIM

"So, Willie, if you're so damn bored, have you ever screwed around on her?" Terrence is eating toast while he speaks into the phone. He sounds bored himself.

"What the hell do you mean?" Willie still feels that he is obligated to sound disturbed.

"Don't be an idiot. You're bored, right? You ever bagged anybody else? Y'know what I mean, a little *slide on the side*?" Terrence is a buddy from college.

Willie feels warm. Sweating. He wants to sound unconcerned. "Well, yeah, I have, dammit. Terry, you know me." He worries that he sounds unstable.

"Yeah I know; that's what I mean—hold it a minute . . ."

Willie can hear Terrence in the bathroom.

". . . sure, sure, you were Mister Fun Guy in college, but that was college. You weren't married yet." Terrence has a cordless phone. The static crackles on the edges of his voice.

"I mean, have you, y'know, fucked anybody in the last couple of years?" Terrence is urinating. Willie can hear the piss rush into the toilet water, gurgling, and then the flat, rain-on-a-tin-roof sound as Terrence guides his stream to the porcelain just above the water line.

"What?!" Willie pulls the receiver from his ear and stares at it. He notices how the off-white hue looks dirty more than off-white. He puts it back to his ear.

"C'mon man!"

"You mean since we've been *married?*" Willie is amazed at how long it takes Terrence to piss. He thinks for a moment that "buddy" is precisely the word he always uses when he introduces Terrence to others, never "friend."

"Well?"

"No. I mean, dammit, I'm supposed to be married, right, asshole?"

"You tell me . . ."

THEM

He felt that she had deliberately guided him into her world of images, but he didn't consider it often. The marriage ran with the same efficiency as doing the month's shopping; as long as she had made out a careful list of what to get, he could bring it home. Sometimes they joked about their sex life being like that and then they would try to laugh as long as they could.

The effort of moving had been such a trial; every possession carried the weight of its investment. At the moment an item was purchased, it seemed essential in the Stills' life. Things like doilies for wine glasses were *always* essential, as if the sun wouldn't shine upon their home without them. There was a root of want in their lives overwatered with a sort of need that was never clearly affirmed or allowed to flourish. And they carried out their existence in the same arranged and reverent manner as they placed the possessions in their home. In retrospect, all of those extra *things* would probably end up being more genuine in the two dollar box of a yard sale ten years down the road.

HER

"It's not that I don't love him. It's not like that at all."

"What do you think it is then?" he says, offering the aspirin. He turns his back to her to get water. He seems unprofessional, back turned, reaching for a glass from the small bar set on the compact refrigerator, but he is listening. He tries to be relaxed for the people that come to see him. He wears sweaters, ties sometimes. He is a very good listener.

"I mean when we have sex, it's pretty wonderful . . . The warmth sometimes is gone, though. That *is* important, isn't it? Warmth . . ." She is nervous.

He hands her the water. "So what do you mean, Helen?"

"Thank you. My head," she sighs.

He nods.

She tries to relax. She remembers that you're supposed to be relaxed. Before she was married, she would get drunk.

"So?" he asks.

"What?"

"What do you mean, Helen?" He is calm. "What do you mean about the sex?"

She is on the verge of sweating. She never talks about sex. But he has given her aspirin and water. And his voice is soothing. Calm. His face has the attractiveness of a priest's.

"I can't help you if you keep your hands bolted to your elbows and your mouth shut. Let's talk this through."

She has looked at him when he wasn't looking at her and she decides that he looks like her brother. But her brother doesn't have the same taste in sweaters. She thinks about how funny her brother's dry humor is. She smiles and her fingers tap at the glass.

"Do you fuck each other, Helen?" He is calm. He knows she is nervous. "Or do you make love?"

She is startled, but she knows it's just a shock tactic. She's read all about it. She says something quickly, but she can't hear her voice. She hopes that she sounds offended.

"What do you do when you . . . make love?"

"Willie's just so damned complacent."

"When you make love?"

"He just doesn't seem to be as deep as I thought he was. I mean—"

"Does he satisfy you?"

"Like the other day, I was trying to figure out where I wanted to put the wicker chairs and he just sat in the yard reading the paper."

"Helen—"

"I mean, it wasn't that the chairs were of any great importance, but we *do* have a whole house to move into, and you'd think that he might want to help."

"How often do you have sex?"

"I suppose it's not like him to be incredibly concerned about things like wicker chairs, but you'd think he could have at least been doing something. I end up doing all of the work and I . . ."

"Who is on top?"

"Sure, sure we both are different and all of that, but after so many years, you get to know a person."

"And?"

"And care for them. I guess. I hate the fact that he

always just follows along. It's never like 'no Helen, let's *not* go out to eat,' or 'honestly, I really *don't* like that chair in that room.' He just follows along. Do you have some more water?" She feels as if she is getting to the core of her problem.

He reaches for the water. His smile is calm, reassuring, but his face shows amusement. "Helen?"

She drinks the water down quickly, spilling some.

"Sometimes . . . sometimes I think I should have seen it before we were married. But he was so *wonderful*, really."

"Helen?"

"My mother always—dammit! I don't know. I do love him. I do. He is good to me, but—"

"Helen."

"What?!"

"Who is on top?"

She tenses. She has tried to play this talking-it-out game. Isn't that what you're supposed to do? You go in, spend your hour, say it's better, and pay the bill.

"OKAY. Dammit, he's a slug in bed! That's it. There really isn't any more to it. Why do *you* people always get so caught up on sex? There *are* other things in a marriage, you know. Sex isn't everything in love. It can't be. I mean, isn't there more to it than that?"

HIM

There are times that he feels he'll just leave. Sure, everybody thinks up that one; not many do it. Like some fad that quickly finds its fashion uncomfortable, it's a passing quirk. But when you really start to feel it. Feel *it,* splintering through you in those tense minutes after work, avoiding her from the mail table to the guest room toilet. Dinners were a practice in well-traveled safe topics over necessary bottles of Pinot Noir. Or there was that thickened silence made obvious by the hectic rhythm of silverware to plate.

Just three weeks in the house and he was telling himself he couldn't breathe. *So leave.* It was times like this, when he felt like leaving, that he was thankful he had never had kids with her yet. *Yet.* Sex quickly came to be a clumsy, fleshy roulette game: no condoms often, no kids yet. But what if he messed up? What then? Then it would be too late. *Leave now.*

He had never been burdened with the tone of off-white in the dining room until she educated him on the mannerisms of light upon certain accepted dining decor colors. He often found himself awake at night, wide-eyed with bitterness and drowning in a sea of colors that bled from the curtains, carpet, and walls into the bed sheets until it was all one overwhelming muddy brown to him.

He needed a cocoon again. College had served him well in that way. There was the folks' summer house outside Boston: an empty place with dust and molding furniture receding into the creaking walls. Or there was his brother Gene's place. Gene's apartment was the genuine-item bachelor cave complete with shaggy dog who probably by now had figured out how to feed itself. That life: no cleanliness, no brassiness, just beer and stacks of *Golf Digest.* The threat of that life was what had drawn him to Helen. But now Willie was considering it: a stasis among islands of empty beer cans, newspapers, and clumps of dog hair that even stuck to the dog. All for the sake of freedom.

The thought that he used to be more free continued to fester. Sitting in the half-moved-into kitchen, he waited for the coffee to drip and he felt sick. He leaned against a stack of boxes packed with dishes and brightly colored towels that he knew would never match that room. Helen would need to get new colors.

What color would you like? These yellow towels just won't work.

I don't know.

*C'mon, Willie. Let's **both** be a part of this.*

White.

White isn't a color, dear. It's just a neutral—

Brown.

Don't be silly.

Blue.

Willie!

Green, dammit.

Mmmm, catchy. Emerald? Or maybe bright olive?

Yellow.

All right, Grumpy, I'll pick the color . . .

His father wasn't much different than this. That thought hit him earlier in the week when he stayed in the bathroom for a half hour, avoiding Helen: *Dammit, Willie, nobody has to shit that long!* But who wants to help decide what wallpaper pattern will go in the study? He was freer before she started cluing him into this whole culture thing. He began to realize how his father lasted all of those years, being fairly intelligent and having an air of refinery, but better suited playing the role of the callous, noncommittal banker. Willie figured his mistake was that he showed he cared too early on in the relationship. His father had been the master of the subdued emotion. All Willie could show for himself was a better paying bank job, a better car, and a forced eye for picking colors.

Not feeling old, but feeling weak, Willie sat down on the floor of the kitchen, realizing that he had always been in awe of the power his father had in *never* showing how much care he invested into anything. Willie, instead, had done so randomly, as if indifference were an emotion. Out of the corner of his eye, he caught the stack of color swatches. *How many shades of goddamn green can someone think up?* He sat there letting the coffee drip, convincing himself that his father would have believed him to be a failure.

THEM

It was important for their friends to know that it wasn't something as petty as the foyer of a damn expensive house that made them buy it. And the neighbors, what about their assumptions? Their curiosity could not be allowed to be satisfied by fabricated rumor. The Stills were ready for this. During the many parties to come, they would tactfully explain away the infatuation with the foyer by baiting others with plans of children to come or the addition of Willie's study onto the living room. For weeks she had rehearsed the responses with him at breakfast. He nodded and threw out the responses sardonically over his coffee. Once he barked and begged for his fish treat and she laughed wildly. She thought the staging of the dialogue to come was fun. It was like improv theater, she said.

HIM

Hello. Hi, Terrence, it's me, Willie.

It's *me*, Terry . . . *Willie*, asshole.

Sorry it's late. I've got to talk to somebody.

Look, I'll buy you a beer sometime. Besides, you're the one who made me so mixed up about this business in the first place.

Well, I finally did it. I've really done it now, dammit. Done what? Terry, I did just what we talked about. Bullshit nothin'. I did.

What?

No, she wasn't mad. She just kind of sighed and told me to tell her again. Y'know, like I would be telling her the truth for real the second time.

Of course I did. Said the same damn thing.

Stop fucking laughing.

Did she break stuff? What kind of question is that? I just told her and—

What? Speak up. Sorry, this phone is kind of messed up. It's old.

Why should I buy a new one? This one is all right. I've had it for years and it's still running, but hey, it's not cordless. Kind of like my marriage . . .

I *said* it's like my marriage. Y'know . . . ?

Yeah, *real* funny. I kill myself.

What?

I said I kill—never mind.

What?

No. I just told you. I told her again and she just looked at me. Then she kind of sighed and turned over and went to sleep.

No, she wasn't pissed. I'm sure. She didn't look like it.

Huh? Speak slower.

That's all. She just turned over and went to sleep.

What did I tell her? What did I *tell* her? What the hell do you think . . . ?

No, I didn't *cheat* on her! Dammit! I told her I *loved* her, idiot.

No. How should I know what's wrong with her? She didn't do anything.

Why? Because I don't think she thought I meant it. She probably thinks I'm holding back.

What the hell do you mean, did I *mean* it?

THEM

"You didn't have to say that, Willie. I mean, not *that*." She rummaged through her small purse for something that she couldn't name right then. It was too dark to see.

He drove. He was silent. He thought about a cup of coffee. And maybe the bathroom. With the newspaper.

"I mean, dammit, no one has to know *all* of our business. Sharon was just being a nice hostess. I mean, dammit!"

"Why would Sharon care why you bought the house?"

"*We* bought that home together dear, remember?"

"Right. What the hell would she care? So what—you like the way the goddamned hallway looks."

"But you don't just *say* that, Willie. I mean . . ."

"Oops, that's right: 'Well, Sharon, dear—oh, I can call you Sherrie?—we bought the house because it will be good for our *goddamn* kids . . .' Was that the proper answer, Helen? Or should I have said something about the neutral colors on the fucking sun porch."

Helen was silent. She shifted in the seat of the car. She realized that she had never liked the feel of the seats in Willie's car. She dug into her purse again. She threw out old tissues and parking tickets, letting them land on the floor.

"Don't get stuff all over the car, Helen." Somewhere in Willie Stills' vision of knowing his father, he felt good in saying that. He thought it sounded like he was in control. He didn't care for Sharon-my-friends-call-me-Sherrie or her party.

Helen felt like saying something, anything that was hurtful. She turned on the light inside the car and began to pick up Taco Bell napkins and old parking tickets. Then she dug for the gum wrappers between the seats. She reached under her seat and pulled out three Coke cans. She looked in the back and fished out pennies from the cushion. A magazine under the floor mat. Gym shorts. And an apple core in the ashtray. She piled them all into her lap.

Willie didn't want to look at her. Looking would be

noticing. He felt a pulling in his chest, the same sort he felt when they went looking for antiques to decorate their new house. He didn't want to look or feel.

When there was nothing else to clean up in the car, Helen swept the length of the dashboard with the sleeve of her blouse. She brought the end of her sweeping arc in front of his face, the sleeve of her Prussian-blue blouse lined with dust. He jerked his head away and pretended that it distracted his driving.

She looked into her lap and sighed. Thick, aged cola oozed out of a can onto her skirt. She picked up her purse and emptied it into her lap, adding to her pile, which brought a quick flash of a satisfied smile. In the last few shakes, with old lint balls and perpetually melting and hardening chocolate mint candies, fell out a crumpled box of cigarettes.

"Oh, William, look! *That's* what I wanted!" They were French and she couldn't pronounce the name correctly, but she remembered liking the color of the box and the smell of the smoke. "Funny me . . . I thought I was going to have to ask you to stop to get some." She pulled out a withered, yellowed cigarette and lit it. It burned quickly. She inhaled noisily, relished it, and then filled the car with bluish-gray smoke. It had been a while, she thought, maybe last fall.

Willie glanced at her. Under a brief flash of streetlights, he saw her smiling through the smoke. He caught himself going over in his mind how he would explain this situation to his father. When he gave up, he stiffened his arms and felt her smile on him.

She laughed to herself because earlier that evening, as they silently got ready for the party, she believed that the tension between them was some new complication because they were in a new home. Moving. *That's all it was,* she had thought. She blew out more smoke.

He thought of coffee. He looked at her, dust-covered, junk-lapped and lost in coils of smoke. "Jesus, Helen."

She smiled.

HERS

"So, Helen, how are you doing today?" He doesn't smile just yet. His sweater is a brilliant yellow, but he is quite concerned. Or at least he wants her to see how concerned he is.

"I think I will have some juice after all. Cranberry?" She feels uneasy, but not out of sorts, not today. Today she is thirsty.

"How are you liking your new place?" He gets her some juice. "The move from mansion to molehill wasn't too much of a step down?"

"Oh, it's nice. Comfortable, in fact. It's taken some time, though. It's a worn, beautifully-weathered little loft with blond wood floors and tall windows every—"

"*And* Helen?"

"But I'll save that for later. Maybe you can see it sometime. I think I'm going to have a Christmas party. A small one. Like five people. Amazing how much money buys so little space. But you never get downtown anyway; you're too suburban."

"And how would you know?"

"Oh, you just look it. Too many Land's End sweaters."

"Funny, funny. And so how do you feel today? How are you doing?" He has not lost the wrinkle above his glasses yet. But he knows she will talk to him now.

"Well," she stops, thinks, breathes, "quite honestly, I'm hungover. I can't believe it. I went out to a nice bar with some friends and, well, I just drank a lot. And this man came up to talk to me. I mean, *me*. And I was drunk. We laughed a lot, but I can't even remember his name. So funny." She laughs and sips cranberry juice. "Maybe I'll go there next week . . ."

"So, what else is going on? How is your job?" His face loosens, unconcerned with the lack of importance in his question. The large void that the house on Morningside Circle had made in her is filling with new, fresh things, he thinks. He smiles, knowing that months ago, still living with Willie, she would respond to his questions with requests for aspirin and compliments about the hue of his sweater.

HIS

> Hello? Hello, Gene?
>
> Hi, it's me. Did I wake you?
>
> What?
>
> It's *Willie*, y'know, your goddamn *brother*?
>
> Yeah, Gene, that's the one. And *only*, tackhead. Hey, man, sorry to wake you, but I just wanted to see if it's still okay to stay at your place for a while. I just can't stand—
>
> What? Speak up.
>
> Oh, no, I'm just ready to move on. This house is just too big, too goddamn much for one stiff to take care of. It looks like a damn museum . . . Well anyway, is it all right for me to stay over there?
>
> I don't know how long.
>
> I'll even clean up.
>
> Just joking. Well?
>
> Hey thanks, Gene. I mean it. I'll see you tomorrow and—
>
> What? What? Say that again, this phone . . .
>
> Oh, okay. Just leave the key under the mat. Thanks. Good night. Oh yeah, Gene, one more thing!
>
> Put the goddamn dog on your porch.

HER. HIM.

The car sat for what seemed too long a time at a stoplight. Neither would let themselves be the first to speak. They waited in silence for the light to change. Mr. and Ms. Stills were moving again.

They were moving, but it would not be as difficult. They both realized that. The yard sale had gone well, although she felt embarrassed most of the day. He drank beer with a forced smile, bargaining away the bits and pieces of years of possession that they had worked themselves into. It had been a warm day and many people came to add the Stills' vases, baskets, towels, and chairs to their homes. He smiled through most of it. It seemed like the upper-hand thing to do. She sat in a wicker chair that was to go on the sun porch and quietly, half-heartedly gave advice on where certain hand towels might look nice. Mostly, she felt worn and cheapened in the presence of neighbors she barely knew.

When they had sold off as much as people would allow themselves to buy, he boxed the rest while she sat in her chair. It had been the fourth day out there, selling away the clutter of their past life. They had wanted to sell it all and felt discouraged in not doing so, even coming together for a moment at the affronting realization that the neighborhood wasn't in envy of everything they possessed. But he was quick to be positive and remind her that living in the neighborhood for only three months was not enough time to get to know their neighbors. Envy takes longer than that, he said. But she was thinking how she never had been in the house next door in the first neighborhood they lived in. They had given that set of neighbors a good four years to grow envious of their teal-colored vases and dried flower arrangements. But neither could ever remember having to go to the china closet to get out extra plates for guests. It had just been the house, the things, and them. Now, years later, and after having locked the door to the second and last house they'd moved into and out of, he put the boxes in the garage for the new homeowners to discover.

He came back dirty with the dust of the things they had not sold. She had offered him a ride to his brother's apartment and he, having sold his car, silently walked to her car and got in. He asked her about the wicker chair, which was still sitting in the yard. She looked at the chair, got into the car, and let it roll out of the driveway before starting it. The chair was beautiful there, white and properly weathered, she thought, perfect against the lush verdancy of the grass. What a vision. Wonderful. Lush. *Hers.* She smiled and whispered, "I know, Mother, 'verdancy' is not a word . . ."

They sat in numb silence, both of them thinking of the future, its out-of-sight-out-of-mind potential. As they rode to Gene's apartment, miles away from Morningside Circle, they came to a traffic light that would not change. When she glanced at him, his fists were clenched on his knees. He looked like he needed to piss. Cars began crossing the intersection, ignoring the stuck light. He mumbled something under his breath. She kept her foot on the brake. She smiled as she thought of that chair. He was ready to be done with all of it.

"Helen, why don't you just go on and *go* through the goddamn light?"

"William . . ." She put the car in park, engine still running, and began to move into the passenger seat, bumping him against the door with her hips. "Why don't *you* drive?"

Leaving the Dog,
I Saw a Buzzard
in the Road

for Lenox,
an old companion

*U*nder lazy oaks and through pestering rain drops, I drove towards a farmhouse on a grassy hill in Georgia, my dog hanging his head out of the car the whole way there. I was taking him to the farm where he had been born. I was taking him there to live out the rest of his years. I couldn't tell if I was sad or just anxious to be done with it.

The ride was both slowly traveled and gone too quickly. The glare of the sun wore on us longer and longer between each grove of shade-giving oak, the hot, baked road, angry and immediate, vaulting us uncomfortably fast towards the promise of each rise where the road rippled in sweltering heat, lost between asphalt and heavy sky. I focused on each horizon of wave-like heat out on the road, feeling drunk and weary with the weight of the moments to come. And the large black Lab in the back, his ignorant tail anxious only about where the car would finally stop.

It had taken minutes. Painful, that thought. We drove up a farm road scarred with ruts and stopped in front of the house. The scene became romantically, sickly obvious as if it were some stolen stroke from a Wyeth or Homer. A gray-haired man smiled from a window and signaled for us to wait while he came from upstairs.

While we waited, my dog and I walked the yard as two young lovers, each one waiting for the other to signify the parting. I had talked to him endless early mornings before, but now words seemed as inappropriate as me expecting him to lick my face one last time. I was not able to care for him properly anymore, and he was in need of so much, so much that even the immensity of this hill and farm and the whole of pastoral Georgia could not contain the instinctive love that he had been born to retrieve and need.

The man came out and smiled at me. He stooped to greet the dog, already rubbing him in his favorite places. I chose to leave quickly after that. As I took the dog bed out of the trunk, I could envision the place where it would sit: in a cozy pantry or next to the man's large roll-top desk. I gave my dog a last pat on the head. Then I rushed to leave, running from his anxious stance and the confused tilt his head always had those times that I drove away without him.

And driving from that farm, I put my hand constantly to my face. I could smell the last time that I rubbed under his neck. My hand had gathered the world of his being, hints of camomile petals and fresh mud from our last walk, the slight suggestion of sassafras and periwinkle hidden away in some fold of bushes or lost patch of wood that I could imagine with smell but never own with my eyes. I held my hand to my face for long stretches of time and wondered what new walks he would now take without me.

That voice was there, telling me I had done what seemed right, but then there was the buzzard, deliberate and slate-colored in the road as I crested a rise. I had to slow down and then swerve, for the bird's posture told me that it did not care what I valued in life. As I went by, it moved sluggishly out of the road as if its affinity to the passing on of life was stronger and more real than mine was able to be.

For a moment, I could envision my reflection in that dark bird's eye. I was vested as the perplexed missionary in the face of his ill-aimed parishioners or the lost child with a goldfish in his hands, realizing that the nature of people, animals, expanses of land and even air itself mock us bitterly and stab at our perception of owning anything that we really didn't create, but, instead, bought or took or were given. We ply our most anxious and confused actions with what we claim the best of intentions, but later, lost in cars on empty by-ways, we find ourselves burdened by those things we call ours, and those intentions slide deliberately away from us drifting slowly, knowingly off the road.

After a few miles, I stopped and tried to hold something of that day in: the green head of the hill, the weathered house crowning it, the patches of blight-wearied hemlocks, the fifteen drops of rain on my windshield, the smell of my hands. The bird.

I sat there, imagining that as I drove away from the farm and from the dog, I heard a gunshot or perhaps the loud crack of a board on something like bones. I imagined that I heard something violent that somehow made me sit more comfortably, as if, by fate, the steel-haired man had decided to kill the dog and by striking it down, fulfilled my childish belief that my ownership of him was the core of his existence and, with our parting, he had no further purpose in living. Maybe I heard this sharp fickle echo.

Or perhaps it was just the falling of a branch in the woods, the screech of late July cicadas, or the gravel under the tires.

As the eye of the bird might have hinted, it was not

a gunshot or a splintering board or the sounds in the fullness of that north Georgia farm.

As I drove away, perhaps I heard some slight rasp of the straining cord that breaks in all of us as we grow older and come to understand how the ownership of things or people, *anything*, is never what makes us live, but clearly marks how painfully we all journey to the grave. I could look back down that road, far off where it lowered and then rose again into dull heat, and wonder where that buzzard was. I could even drive back, come upon it, still in the road, and replay my swerving over and over, turning the wheel less and less each time. Each time hoping to connect with that bird, the sound that I was still hoping to hear and the heat that was still pushing me to move quickly away, always, always, away.

The Trip Back
from Whidbey

for Jason and our father

Without bitterness, Maya could remember watching the two on the beach with that dog. She thought of that time as she now sat on the sloop, watching the space of water widen between her and the island. It was a different beach back then, different driftwood, a younger tree line of blue spruce, and thousands of low tides ago. In those long ago mornings she watched Joe and little Terry trudge off through the fog, nettles, and ripening blackberry bluffs. Often she stepped out to the porch an hour later and charted their progress on the beach far below. From way off she could make out their figures, Terry in red galoshes stumbling after Otis, wet already, soon to deposit his canine smell in the pantry for the rest of the week. And Joe, ambling along hundreds of feet behind them, his smooth, deep-brown forehead to the sky. He had smoked pipes back then. When Terry and the dog circled back close enough, sometimes he would try to tackle them both and allow them the fun of barely escaping. Hours later they were back, boots full of water, grinning and tired as they peeked in at her over the sill of the kitchen window.

Otis was always immediately ushered to the back

porch, barking for more play and with no ear for the light-hearted scolding she'd give the boys, father and son, for staying out too long. All three must have known she was faking it. By bedtime Joe would be standing on the porch petting Otis and making up excuses as to why Terry would sleep more comfortably with the dog in his room. That silly old brown dog: saliva everywhere, a coat of curious white splotches like he'd stumbled into some house painter's ladder. Laughable, enjoyable animals, the three of them.

Sometimes she thought Joe and Terry had forgotten that she, too, had come to the island for a vacation. Day after day, they'd be out there again, and she would be alone, watching, not even sad, just there, like the novel that stays in the beach bag the whole trip. It was a different beach then.

Now as the sloop headed for the mainland, she was thinking of that beach as she last saw it an hour ago from the water. As the sloop slid away from Whidbey, she hugged herself, remembering. She could hear Joe messing with his thermos.

"Maybe you shouldn't drink quite yet, Joseph." She wasn't looking at him; she focused on their wake. "The whitecaps are high all the way in."

But his hand stayed on the thermos of bourbon. Pressed against the starboard rail, his outline sharp in the gray of a spent sky, he maneuvered the sloop's tiller as an afterthought. *He will be like this all the way into Everett,* she thought, and decided that the nap she wanted would have to wait. She crossed the cockpit and stood next to him for a while, thinking she would be warmer there. Even in summer, these erratic Pacific inlet winds surprised her skin. Wind was insistent, the salty blast of the Puget Sound swirling around them.

Maya remembered another time Joseph and she had been on the sloop weathering the cool wind current that crept around the northeastern tip of Whidbey and picked up speed as it made its brisk race towards the mouth of the Columbia River. Terry had decided to stay on shore, collecting agate, so Maya and Joseph had taken this day sail alone. It was time to turn the sloop back in, but they had half a bottle of wine left and the sun hung above the horizon so brilliantly red that they felt it would be wrong to let it slip into the water unnoticed. Joseph had secured the tiller, taken off his shirt, and held her for a few moments, making her feel almost too warm, deep in her chest and at the edges of her ears. Smiling shyly, saying nothing, he lay her down onto spread quilts and undressed her slowly, exchanging her pullover for the blankets of cool mist that drifted over the sloop. But when he was inside her, she wasn't cold. She took in the silence of the open water, the warmth between their waists and again that fire in her ears. Amidst the lapping of the waves, she felt a thick, full sort of silence, and they warmed each other's faces with their breath, not moving or gyrating, but letting the sway and soft dip of the vessel, adrift on the waves, move them slowly in and out, apart and together. Their hips ground at some moments and, at others, were together, but motionless for long stretches, waiting for the next wave. They stayed like that until dark, and even after they were both tired and had been lulled in and out of sleep by the motion of the waves, she lay under him, warmed by his weight while he caressed her face, singing silly variations of old sailing songs from a cassette that she had bought him as a joke at the ferry port in Everett. On the way in she sat at the prow, giggling like a young girl at the soft whisper and random squeak of his singing voice.

Thinking of that time, she turned to him, offering the brush of her breast against his arm. He remained focused on the motion of the wheel and the thermos in his hand. Still, she tried to hold him.

"Please, Maya." His body braced.

She pulled away, zipped up her jacket to the chin and sat opposite him.

"Why don't you go below and check the bag," he said with a pulling in his voice. "The fur. It might be getting wet."

"I don't think I want to do that right now."

"It shouldn't get wet. The fur will smell."

She didn't answer, but again concentrated on the wake of the sloop, the foam lines quickly being rolled into themselves over autumn-eager Puget Sound waves. *He won't say 'Otis,'* she thought. Otis as a name wouldn't do much good anymore. Otis had become an *it*. His smell would never linger in the pantry of the island house again.

Whidbey Island still was visible, beyond where the wake fanned out, and she convinced herself that she could make out the docks and beach fronts just north of Mukilteo. In and out of coming late-day gray, up and down among the waves, the green head of South Whidbey lulled her into visions of the driftwood in tide pools, agate scattered along the western beaches, salt-frosted evergreens, twisted and old, and a stinging realization that the summer had been cut short.

They had planned this as their last stay on Whidbey. The end of August was looming ahead and they were still recovering from the loss of Terry leaving early for college. She knew that their son's departure had been especially hard on Joseph. Terry left just months after Joseph's company had decided to cut back and had let him go first. She spent many nights since then alternating the direction of her support between her husband and her son, entertaining Joseph in the absence of their only child and reassuring him that the company didn't let him go because he was Black or because he wasn't good. She had held him sometimes as if he were her only child, and each time figured out new ways to say that even good people have bad times.

The Trip Back from Whidbey

This was to be the last good summer or perhaps the last *rich* summer. Joseph had been persistent in pointing that out. He figured that his plan for a new job at a community center in Tacoma would not allow room for luxury expenditures, boats, summer homes, and unnatural airs.

Terry seemed to handle well the news of Joseph being let go. He was off to spend the first of his college years, and his parents had done well to save for it. The concern was not his. But Joseph had worried on the late nights of that summer. Waiting for Terry to come home from parties with his prep school friends, he would sit in the den, rubbing Otis' belly, feeling defeated. Where, *why* was Terry going, he would ask Maya, so far from him and breaking away from roots he had worked so hard to cultivate. He'll be Black whether he goes to Stanford, Oxford or Bob Jones University, Maya had told him. He wouldn't get any more aware of himself by living under Joe's arm forever. But she knew that the times father and son had spent together would not wash so easily from Joseph.

This trip to Whidbey had been truly liberating, just as they planned, she thought. Joseph was starting to accept Terry's absence and fall back into his yearning for the beach and the summer cottage. They even joked about the life that they had been living, her teasing him about their vacations being "convenient bourgeois departures" from their true selves. He laughed along with her, but she knew how hard it was for him. It had taken years for him to justify to *himself* a life that allowed things like the cottage on Whidbey Island, even as he was trying to impress upon Terry the danger in attaching too much importance to objects. It was difficult parenting for him. The Blacks Joseph knew—even Blacks he'd never known—just didn't sail off into the Puget Sound to beach houses.

With her acceptance of the cottage on Whidbey as

being far from luxurious, but definitely not rustic, she took to playfully baiting him and his modified sensibilities. Joseph was the one who first mentioned the idea of the cottage. For all of his lessons to Terry in the ways of social class and the have-nots of life, the cottage's facilities offered chances for harmless satire for Maya. She had not minded it really, nor had Terry who, in their first summer at Whidbey, was too young to understand what irony was. Through the years Maya became quite accustomed to their accelerated sense of standards.

But that had been some years back and their luxury had become an uncomfortable garment to wear, especially now that she would have to remove it. She tried not to let herself get bitter, now leaving the island and a vacation stolen from her by the death of a dog and Joseph's strange preoccupation with getting it back home.

She looked from the island to the single mast of the sloop, now faded from its original brilliant white. Below it the carelessly stowed jib had been thrown. Gray and like an invalid creature it appeared now, tucked away from those younger years when they first bought the sloop and Terry was too young to be allowed anywhere above deck except between Joseph and the wheel. *We're not even using the wind on the way in,* Maya thought, *not even this last time,* and she felt cheated of that sensation. Seeing the age of the bare mast, how ironic and foolish this garment of luxury seemed to her now.

Sometimes she had to think for a moment to remember her old self, her legs still a soft, smooth brown, taut and unversed in the ways of a wet deck dancing with the Puget Sound currents. She stared at the barren mast and laughed quietly. She was remembering a dirty joke Terry made about his dating problems as he leaned against the mast a few years back during his confused summer of sixteen. Then, too, it

The Trip Back from Whidbey

was tall and bare, but less worn and, evidently by its presence and place in time, more humorous. She remembered how Joseph had laughed, giggling with his son, more as a good friend than a father. She allowed herself a soft, tickled laughter.

"You say something, Maya?"

"No, just remembering something." But she could see the inappropriateness of this. It would not help matters. Laughing. Or remembering. Earlier that summer, she had tried humor to lighten the preparation for how their life would be changing. She'd tried jokes about eating rice every night and having unframed pictures of the sailboat they *used* to have taped to their small economy refrigerator.

But Joseph, despite her kidding, held fast to his social commitment. He felt empowered in letting go of this romance of things to return to a world, his world, of serving necessity in peoples' lives more so than want in his own. She remembered the hurt he displayed when she teased him in front of Terry. It was important to Joseph that his son understand that being more wealthy and affluent never had to mean being less Black and that there was no shame in knowing your background, or as Joseph seemed proud in considering, returning to it. This was especially important. At random times Joseph held Terry gently by the wrist or shoulders, emphatically solid, telling him *don't forget me. Don't forget where you came from.* And in the summer before Terry's senior year of high school, Joseph had begun pressing into him the concept that you don't, *you can't,* run from your origins; it's not good to hide them. Even if you think you're secure in clothes or boats or houses. Or a well-paying job. Or at a prestigious college in California, far, far away from your parents.

She felt a private bitterness at Joe's stoicism and how the turn of events after he was fired did not come upon them unfortunate and overwhelming like some sudden squall, but more deliberately, planned out, and painfully prepared for by him. The summer and winter trips, the house, and even some of the furniture were to go; "necessary relinquishings," he termed them. He hadn't been eager in the job search and the prospect of service at the Tacoma community center loomed closer. Fate hadn't been dealt out to them. He had *chosen* it. They were to make room for the change.

She felt the wind in her face. Whidbey was no longer in sight, only him, framed in the gray sky. She turned her shoulders eastward toward Everett, where, if he had been more lighthearted and kept the sail up, they might have reached before the pier lights began to flicker in the coming dark. But he had lowered the main sail soon after they rounded the tip of Whidbey and resigned himself to a solemn stance at the wheel, guiding the sloop under auxiliary power through the choppy waves. It was hard to be bitter. That took energy. It was selfish; she knew he would say that if he could see the sullen look in her face.

Affirming this herself, she felt obligated to comfort him. She made a gesture with her arm towards the withered jib. "I remember when I didn't even know what a goddamned *jib* was." She tried a smile. "And *sloop*. Remember *that* one, Joe? You must have read up; you sounded like somebody's ole sea dog: *'Maya, go ahead and put—'* or was it 'stow?' Yes: stow . . . 'stow the bags in the sail locker . . .' and I said something like *'but I thought we're driving the* boat *out there.'"* She laughed loudly, pleased she could laugh at herself. "That was something."

But he had taken out a cigarette and was concentrating on cupping his hands to light it.

"And look at us now," she said, letting her laughter fade. Facing east again, she saw a few lights along the steely evergreen shore of the mainland.

He let the smoke curl around his head and he winced into the wind in a manner that she noticed he had taken on in the recent summers of sailing. "So you're really not going to go down and check on the bag?"

"No, I'm not. There's not much more we can do about him."

"It's just the fur, Maya. It shouldn't get wet. And if air gets to the skin . . ."

"Let's just not . . ." She closed her eyes tight with a knotted sense of resolve, an insulating kind of blocking out which she allowed as a necessity. "Let's not talk about it anymore."

"You'll have to do better than that when Terry sees him."

"You can't be serious about driving that dog's body all the way to Stanford."

He focused his eyes on Everett and reached under the wheel console for the thermos of bourbon.

"Are you going to check the bag for leaks at every rest stop?" She knew her voice might sound cruel right then to him. "And what about the smell? Are you going to keep Otis on ice for a *thousand* miles?" But she felt vindicated and fueled with the sense of being the more rational one.

He drank slowly from the thermos, heaving air out after the bourbon had gone down.

"Joe, please, it's rough all the way in. You know the current from Saratoga Pass. Why don't you rest and let me steer?"

He said nothing. He didn't move.

She heard the waves for the first time since they had left the island. She listened to their gentle pat and splash as she hadn't in years.

He finally spoke. "We'll fly him."

"Fly? Fly *Otis*?! Dammit, Joseph!"

He pulled his face back into that wince again. "Please, Maya . . ."

She decided that she hated his face with that wince. And the insipid *please Maya*. She felt that this was his way of pushing the pain onto her.

"Terry," he said.

"What?"

"We'll fly *Terry* up."

"So, Joseph, we're into flying again? Can our wallet stand that? What happened to commutes and treks in our soon-to-be acquired VW Bus? Or was it a rickshaw?"

"Jesus, think of Terry. He said he wanted to see . . ."

Otis had been old, and for his nine years had been the mellowed companion on all of their trips to Whidbey. She knew this. But Otis was gone now.

"A goddamned *dog* keeps us in luxury. I'll be damned."

"You don't have to help with the arrangements if you don't want to."

"Joe, you give up our only time together this year for a dead dog?"

His wince broke for a moment and she could see that too much had been said. His stoicism would not take that.

"I just want to do this." He drank again. "For Terry." His face set back into a gaze towards the shore.

It wasn't just the dog. It was difficult to have Terry leave early for school. But an apartment had to be found, a cheap place found early, and so Terry went. Maya could remember Joseph seeing the brighter side of their son's early departure. He told her that the last time on Whidbey would be theirs alone, echoing back to when she had first dated him and learned to love him there, when they could only afford the ferry and two days in a motel. This was to be a last good stay, not an event tainted by a slow, heavy trip back to mourn. But it wasn't just the dog.

The Trip Back from Whidbey

Otis had passed away in a manner that, to her, seemed fitting. They had been on Whidbey for a day, good weather in the coming week promised by forecasters, and they had already begun an expedition for mussels. Otis had broken off in his regular fashion, forever enthused with being simply a dog and emphatically determined to herd seagulls from the beach. If one could assign emotion to a dog, or even importance, she felt that Otis was happiest trotting along the beaches of the Sound, his tongue hanging out. One moment Otis had been chasing gulls as Joseph and she were shoulder to shoulder, digging like children for a large mussel burrowing away from a future in their stew pot. They lost the mussel in wet, sliding sand and they slumped back on their heels. And there he was. Otis had collapsed without them even knowing, without sound, without struggle. She gasped first. Remembering that now, she thought of reminding Joseph of this, as if her shock then might impress upon him that, yes, she did care for Otis. But it was Joseph who walked over, picked up the body and walked slowly to the house. Even then, his face was sinking into the drawn, hard look it held now.

They didn't call a vet. That seemed fitting, too, and they sat in the kitchen that night, silent, drinking both of the bottles of wine they had brought. The oil lamp light punctuated the weight of Joseph's withdrawn appearance. His face, his hands, and even his clothes seemed to have taken on some silt or grime of gray after he carried the dog to the cottage. That night, Otis lay in a bag covered with ice on the porch.

They had been silent that night, but she had sensed that he was already thinking of Terry's reaction. The next morning she heard Joseph on the phone with his son. She heard talk of the dog for a brief time, but then Joseph focused more on the time passed and Terry, his son, so far away. She imagined Terry, tired, maybe even irritated, being treated like the son Joseph still wanted him to be. She sat on the bed, watching the deep blue of the morning lighten to gray and listened to Joseph in the kitchen trying not to cry. By noon he had packed, and she stumbled into him as he passed the front steps carrying a white styrofoam cooler down to the dinghy. He said he had walked to the store and bought it for Otis, for the trip back. For Terry, he had said.

It was more, she realized now. She had always been put off by his sensitivity that, in showing care for delicate issues, appeared impressive. Earlier, as he let down the main sail, she hated him for his look of resolve, just as she had hated how he would wear his frayed Peace Corps shirts to picnics and beach parties, signifying the sacrificial glory of his days in eastern Africa. He sometimes wore his pain like it was heavier upon him than her.

But she had heard a difference in his voice just then. . . . *for Terry*. It was now about more than the trip back. She thought of the day Joseph hugged Terry tight, longer than he would usually allow his son to take notice of, and watched Terry walk away to board his plane. Terry was now gone, left to the unknown design of his own life. Home became a desperate place, a little more silence in the house, and those still, lonely fall months coming. There was no way to know how much of their eighteen years together he would take and what he would leave.

"We can call Terry when we get in." She rose and took the bourbon from him. She saw tired pain on his face, and his shoulders loosened when she touched him.

Somewhere in California Terry was smiling and getting his brown skin darker, oblivious to the passing of a dog, the weight of things changed, life reverting.

"The piers are getting close, Joe," she said softly, letting him sit down. She no longer felt cold. She took the wheel and quieted the motor to let the sloop drift for a while towards the lights of Everett.

Sister Got a Man

for Brothers everywhere

*T*hough he couldn't quite remember when, there came a time Shorty grew to hate beating his wife. It wasn't the brutality of leather or knuckles on flesh, but the silence, the noiselessness of withered feelings. And he couldn't figure out whose feelings, either. He'd come in after nights out with Reggie and Ed and stumble into the front door of his real-life world, at home. In the stillness of foul whiskey-sweat air he grew to dread the solitary sound of the beating. Sylvie would no longer cry. *Cry, goddammit, say sumthin'. . .* The sound, a rhythm of distancing in the open-fisted blows, forcing itself onto her skin, but not into her body.

It wasn't a big thing around the fellas. A conversation piece to be stepped around, but sort of like everyone knew. *Say, Shorty, how's your lady Sylvia doin'? I mean, she still cook greens good an' all, don't she?*

And Sister, Sylvie's friend, with her late night drunken visits, stepping in on them, her biting comments as she helped herself to the liquor. The tone of her voice: a passing-off of the issue with an oh-don't-pay-no-never-mind-to-me-Shorty attitude. And her eyes. The eyes: cutting. *I don't care what you do to her; your woman, your problem, not mine.* Small comments, words as persistent as the rhythm. And him always asking himself, *Shorty, just what the fuck wrong wit' you, man?* as if his body was someone else's.

But usually he would pass it off, joking in a bar or drinking on Reggie's back porch. Or at the ball courts. Whenever Reggie wasn't killing his liver and Shorty wasn't at home beating his wife. *Brother Shorty: the 'family man.'*

It was all left to laughing. Just laughing, as the fellas tended to do.

Sometimes after work, Reggie, Shorty and Eddie sat on the porch and drank themselves into conversations about their lives and their women. *If I could ever get to figgerin' out that woman, I might even be home some of the time,* Reggie would breathe into his glass, *'tween her an' the bossman, I ain't got much left of my ass.* All they did was laugh. Talking and laughing. Drinking. *Yeah, Reg', I suppose you right. . . .* And keeping silent. A musty porchful of silence that divided the sips of liquor and the sighs of tired, dark men.

Often, because he was too drunk or too scared to get started, Shorty was the quietest of the fellas, laughing when Ed made a joke about someone's wife or waving his glass, bourbon spilling, agreeing whenever Reggie began to ramble about how to fix things in his life that had broken long ago. *An' I'll tell you what, Eddie . . . That man—you know—that sucker, Johnson? Well he need to take his narrow little ass on in there and have it out with the bossman. Acks Shorty, he know . . . Ain't I right? Sho I am. The Man ain't givin' nuthin' an' Johnson ain't said shit for us. Bump that noise, brother. Hell, I got haf a mind to go on in there mysel' . . .*

Shorty would nod, sipping and waving his whiskey, trying not to say much of anything. He wondered if it was just that Reggie was full of it—no schooling past tenth grade and too much smart ass past that—or was it just that you

78

don't go against the fellas, take their word and they'll take yours? Or was it just that he was afraid that they would start in on him if he said something? *Damn, Shorty, you fixin' to get real now? You startin' in? Well hell, nigger, what's all this biz'nis with you an' your lady . . . what about* that? *Well alright then, just stay light on the words . . .* And it was all laughs. And Shorty would stay silent. *Just smile. Just laugh with 'em, dammit. Just drink, be silent. Keep your hands on your cup, keep your hands feedin' you drinks, keep 'em still, keep 'em from smackin' that sucker . . .* He would hold it in. Save the energy. Hold the fists. Save it. Tonight, at home, he would use it.

Tonight he was driving his cab home from the bar, late. Thursday night: something special about Thursdays, his mother used to say. He'd drive with Reggie from the garage and they'd meet Eddie and the others at the park for mens' league basketball. The park glistened at dusk, the benches, broken bottles, metal backboards, the slick of courts, all playing with the light. And the brown, bare skin, moving, flowing, wearing themselves out for a night's glory, a moist hug, a sense of being something, someplace.

They had come here Thursday nights for as many years as they could play ball. They were good, too; had shirts made, name on the back, matching shorts, clean sneakers. You had to come out there to win, looking like it, playing like it. But it was more than the look that got you on the court in style. It was the skill, the run of your game that brought you presence, domain. They no longer had the speed or spin-and-drive flow of years back, but their moves were refined to a precision dealt out with look-away passes, decade-old crossover dribbles, and an affinity for the court and for each other that made the ball seem made especially for their victories. Shorty loved it. Even though Shorty had played forward in school, Reggie always subbed him in at guard. *Shorty man, your shit get blocked too damn much.* But Shorty handled it. And he handled the game. He knew the game. *Ain't nobody 'blocked' them eight three-pointers last week. Fifteen, twenny-five, thirty feet. Anyplace. It was all 'money' shots* . . . Sometimes it felt like it was all his.

Afterwards, in the bar they'd get drinks and sit behind the pool table watching the women and younger men come in. There in the dark, they watched younger images of what they were. *Jive-ass kids, got no damn sense.* The fellas knew what was going to happen. They watched the young men drinking themselves into age, fooling into a frustration that they wouldn't notice until later on.

Shorty could remember good times, spent drinking lightly, just beer back then, playing pool on the new table with the live bumpers and a new hole from one of Eddie's abandoned cigarettes.

Tonight Shorty was leaning against the table, thinking about when *he* used to watch the men behind the pool table. He put his dark, weathered hands onto the felt. He pressed down and he could feel the age of the hard surface, its lumps and warped places resisting his hands. He pressed harder. The tips of his fingers grew cool. With the urgency of needing to escape a feeling he couldn't name, he stepped back from the rail. He stood up, bolt-straight, attentive to empty space. He looked around to see who might have seen him. He looked at the table and imagined the way the old, worn cloth must feel. Then the sweat hit him.

"Somethin' grab yo' ass Shorty?" Eddie laughed from behind him.

"No. Naw, naw, jus' got a chill or sumthin'." Shorty stooped into the slant of the light over the table and ran his hand along the bumper. He squeezed it. He scratched at the rougher, worn areas. The music from the jukebox played a heavier bass than he remembered; the lights must have been dimmed, the air-conditioner not on high enough. Nothing much was different—maybe the newer songs mixed with the old—but the air and the lighting, the low ceiling and deep red walls of the place had not changed. Perhaps the place was smaller. He felt a closeness, like he'd pushed himself into a closet filled with old winter clothes.

Reggie got up, speaking loudly. He was balancing his drink with a blurred faith and had the fellas laughing at some story about the time he made it with one of the waitresses right on the pool table. "Hell, that ain't no goddamn liquor stain on that felt, brother!"

Shorty felt it was good to laugh at stories. Stories were good to think of. They all tried this ritual of forgetting at one point or another. Reggie usually was the best at trying to forget. Or at least, if one ever helped the other, he was the best drinker.

"*Say*, hey you! Hey girl, git up off them heels an' rest on over here. Hey, *baby*, how you? C'mere, woman!" Some nights, Reggie didn't even remember his wife's name. "Naw, baby, c'mon back. See, you got me all wrong; jus' want a cuddle . . ."

"Say, man—Reggie . . . Reg', listen. Sit down," Shorty shouted, trying to help Reggie out. "Ah, what you want to drank?"

"Some of that *ass*, Shorty. Shit, man, mine your own biz'nis, I'm tryin' to get some—hey, *hey!* Girl, c'mere. Shorty, you get your biz'nis t'gether and I'll get mine. Say what, girl? . . . shit . . . go on then . . . didn't need you anyhow; shit, I got my own damn wi-"

As usual, when Reggie sat back down, Shorty got him another drink. After so many years, or drunk nights out, Reggie would confuse the two: a woman he didn't love and a life he hated. But facing it, being made to face it, Reggie was just a man, like most, like all of them. Everybody had limits. After a while, Reggie would lift his head to look at them. He took sips from ice water in his glass, just staring at them, facing his friends, men just like him.

"Don't look at me like that. You know how it is, Eddie? *Shorty?* Don't give me that shit. Jus' lookin' for some fun, for *somethin'*. The Man ain't never give me nuthin', an I got to enjoy what I can. Don't tell me you ain't doing the same." His eyes lowered and his voice retreated. "Hell. Jus' drank."

Shorty would laugh about it, laugh with the fellas, with Reggie, at him. He had laughed earlier tonight. But in his cab, now, driving home with his "on-call" light on for no reason, he didn't feel like laughing. At times like this, when he was alone, he began to see how small he was. How small they all were. *Little men . . . you ain't the big man, brother . . . jus' a fuckin' little, little man.* He thought back on all of the nights in that bar and the pattern that they made. All those times had brought a certain grayness to their smiling faces. But they never saw it as a problem, just a mood to be washed over. In the cab, removed from the bar, even the good moments began to lose color.

"Shorty, brang us the dranks 'fore we forget we supposed to be drankin'." Reggie had yelled out earlier that night.

Shorty stood there in the middle of the room, feeling his face. It took him a few seconds to figure out if they were laughing at him or whether they were really that drunk already. Or was he drunk? Was he slow? Was he really "Shorty" at all? Was he the goddamned "big man?" *Stupid ass negro . . . stop foolin' . . . get on home boy, get on home . . .*

"Say, *Shorty*, hurry your ass up!" Now Eddie was getting drunk.

Shorty. Sometimes it was just the name.

"C'mon, brother, you about as slow as you is on the court." *Shorty*. It was probably Reggie who gave him the name, or Sister, his wife's friend. She was like that; slow on kindness and quick on lighthearted insult. The kind of humor that cuts because it's true. Yes, it was Sister, Shorty thought. Another night, other drinks, different reasons to drink them.

"Shorty, get the hell over here. Damn ice is meltin'." Shorty had been staring at himself in the bar mirror. *Shorty . . . As if I'm the small one. Bigger than Eddie, shit. I ain't even that short . . . just a sucker. Hell, I got the 'money' shot. I'm the big man . . . I'm the . . .* Laughing. He looked at them. *Niggers laughing.* Laughter all around him in the dark. He picked up the tray of drinks and shuffled his best "Unca Tom" shuffle over to the fellas who bent over in laughter. *Laugh, motherfuckers.* Shorty could always make them smile. He had done it dozens of times before. *Good time fella, funny-ass nigger, hah! He look jus' like . . . Hey Shorty, do that shit again.* And it was as if there wasn't enough laughter in the whole place to make him smile. . . . *get on home boy.*

They had laughed and drank and smoked, but they couldn't leave. After another drink, he had thought, it'll be alright, it always is after another drink. *I don't need to go home . . .* Maybe Shorty would forget the way home for once. Maybe he could act like Reggie, running around through the smoke and darkness, looking for someone to love him . . . *I don't got to go home . . .*

He heard the commotion of other men getting on Reggie about messing around with the girls at the pool table. Reggie had been trying to forget the way home, too. Shorty had a bad feeling that he wasn't as drunk as he wanted to be. He remembered his own wife at home, probably sitting up with Sister, getting drunk. And for a moment, he got mad. He sipped his drink.

"Aw, hell, fellas, if a man can't have no fun sometime, why spend time at all? Now look there, Eddie, Shorty: take that lady over there. Now see, she needs to be mines tonight." Shorty looked across the room wondering if he was drunk enough. He drank the last out of his glass. He would have another.

And then later that night, as Shorty turned the cab onto his street, he could almost laugh, yes laugh, wondering why a voice in his head had said 'go home' and why, even after another drink, he had listened. Maybe around 1:30 he found himself a little drunk, a little lost, a little like Reggie, laughing with the fellas and starting to think about how it feels to touch a young woman; around 1:30 a.m., maybe a woman who isn't your wife.

Shorty slowed the cab and remembered laughing hard, almost on the floor, glad of the crack he'd made about the words "young" and "woman" having nothing to do with "wife." And he didn't really know who was laughing with him; it didn't matter. They all felt it. Some just handled it better. And some, like Reggie, well . . . that was Reggie. Reggie could never even say "wife" without choking. He pulled the cab to the curb, hoping Reggie and Eddie had found their curbs, too. *Take it light, brother.* Shorty smiled, remembering the warmth of Eddie's drunken goodbye. Usually, he dropped Eddie off, but Shorty had left early, that voice pushing him home. And now it was that same voice closing in on him in the car. He sat there, rubbing the wheel, engine running, brake pedal down, lights on, not moving.

If things were different, perhaps if it was cooler, early spring maybe, he might feel different. Thinking about how it feels when it's April was a way to remember, without pain, home, being a boy and being his mother's son. Thinking about April helped him remember when he felt better than he did right at that moment. He would trick himself with fantasies like this to justify his immobility.

With a rag from his pocket, he began to dust off his dashboard. Even at night, even when he felt like this, even on a low Thursday night, he could shine up his car. He got out and worked on the front. He caressed it, hugged the hood as he reached for the tough spots. His waist and thighs knew the curved places well. The smooth roundness where the sides rushed from their flare into the headlights was still warm against his thighs. *Look at that chrome. My shit look good. My baby look damn fine.* His hot, sweet, whiskey breath steamed the grille. He grasped the chrome, rubbing it, pressing the cloth to it, making it glow. He had chosen the chrome fixtures and put them on himself. They were a gift to himself when he made the last payment on the cab. For all of its size, roundness, and age, the cab belonged to him. It was really the only thing that he felt he owned, that he controlled.

It felt good having that car. It was his. Eddie always talked about having some worth if you had some place or something to call your own. He hadn't chosen his name, Shorty thought, but he owned his cab. Sometimes not getting out of the car was easier than walking into the house. Flickering streetlights above kept life simple on the street. The blue, timeless lights shining down, making the shade on his skin and the shadows around the car one hue.

He had been silent tonight as they talked about the young women at the bar that would make good wives. Most of the qualifications had to do with the tightness of the pants, the red lips, the length of nails, the lack of commitment.

"Hell, Shorty, you could marry *Sister,* hah!" Reggie had said. "She'd love you right, what with them hips she got and the way she dance: *Man!*"

"That ain't too goddamn funny, Reggie," Shorty's voice was strained.

"Let me get you another drank, brother, jus' messin'. But you are always talkin' 'bout that woman, hell I just figured . . ."

Shorty's stare led Reggie to the bar-rail.

"Man got to wonder sometime if he made a mistake, Short. I mean, Sylvie's nice an' all, but . . . well . . ." Reggie backstepped to the bar.

Shorty glared.

Eddie took in a large sip. "Hell, the same ole' woman can't be lovin' *that* good every night. Know what I'm sayin'?"

Shorty allowed a laugh and Reggie came with more drinks.

"Well, okay, Shorty, who would you marry if you could marry anybody?"

Shorty stopped laughing. He got silent the way you quiet down after no one laughs at the joke you've told. As he was about to open his mouth to boast about a fling with the red dress three tables over, he looked down at his fingers, the left ones. He just stared at them, eyes tired from cloudy visions of possession, as if the gold band was a symbol of freedom. As if he had that much control in the matter. As if that thin band of gold was like the big rings those Vikings wore that he read about when he was a kid. He used to read a lot about them; they were his favorite. Vikings: free, raging, raping, traveling, wearing gold everywhere, showing their power. *You can't never be no Viking no how,* his daddy would say from a vodka half-sleep in his easy chair, *you'd look a damn fool growing White folks' red hair. 'Sides, niggers can't wear that much gold, no how: get their ass shot.* Shorty had tried to figure out the connection between his father's outlook and the way things really were. His face almost gave away how confused he was, but he was good at looking like he was thinking about the depth of the question. *If you really had your choice, who would you marry, Shorty?* And that ring: as if a gold band were a symbol of unbending freedom and, at the same time, as if it meant he were bound to something. Or was he?

Now, sitting next to his cab, he remembered how long the silence seemed to last while the fellas waited for an answer. And their amazement at how fast he could take down half of his double bourbon, his slurps and the tumbling ice breaking the silence.

In the blue of the street light, the gold band shone less warm. Just then he realized how the fellas had looked at him in the bar, him with his head down, never answering their question. *Leave, man, just leave. But don't go home.* Sitting on the curb, he watched the headlight rays sink into the dented trash cans ahead. He looked up to the house and then back to the cans. He smiled. He remembered some crazy saying of his mother's about the joy of having a house to come home to. But being home was different. Being home was too much, too real. The trap of dealing with Sylvie. *Please say somethin' tonight . . . please . . . say somethin', dammit.*

The lights were on inside and he could see movement, shadows from the T.V. glare. Two figures: Sylvie's and the taller, larger-breasted silhouette with newly done hair from Gracie's Doo Boutique. Sister. He could tell her without the hair or the figure. He knew before he even got out of his car. He had to park at the curb because his space in the driveway was taken. There it was, the gray Bonneville, white walls and one shiny hubcap. And then looking into the house, he still knew: Sister's shadow would have the bottle. She wouldn't be going home tonight, he thought. The booze always made sure of that. *Won't even be able to talk to my own goddamn wife.* He thought of Sister on the couch later in the evening, talked out and passed out again, Sylvie on the floor, both of them taking up space. He tried to figure out what he was going to say when he got inside, when he walked into his own house and felt like leaving.

He thought of the chairs on the back porch. He'd slept there before. *Should just tell her to get on home. Hell, it's my damn house. Just get the hell out! That's what Reggie'd tell the bitch.* But Shorty knew better than that. There was no telling Sister. She had her way, her *own* way with everything. He couldn't even remember when she first began to fill his house with her deep-throated laugh. He just got used to it. Maybe it was ever since Sylvie met her at the bar a while back. Or maybe it was way back when Eddie thought he could make a fine man for Sister. Whenever that was, if he'd known how to deal with her then, he thought, things would be different. He rubbed his face. If he could have dealt with any woman—his real sister, his mother—back when he was a kid, it would all be different. He could look down the street and almost see where the frustration might have begun. Looking down a few blocks, through the blue lamp haze, straining to make out the older houses and seeing back into memories of them, the places where he was raised.

Just about this time of year, Miss Eula's patches of lilies would bloom and he remembered a hiding place among them where he would sit for hours, waiting for his momma's ass-beating arm to grow calm. And the lilies across from his old house. Spring days along that street were ablaze with the fierce yellow-orange of the lilies and hints of heat to come. The thought of flowers didn't comfort him anymore; seeing and thinking of the lilies always pushed him into terrible memories of hot Sundays, his mother and his sister.

On those Sundays he would go with his momma and his sister to his auntie's for supper. And they always had to take lilies. Orange day lilies. Nothing else and, of course, she wouldn't like them unless they were wrapped in that green, crunchy tissue from the flower store. It was a race between his sister and him to find the best blooms.

Get on out there and pick them lilies, chile. Don't want no wilted ones neither, hear? He had to pick the good stalks; the bad ones wouldn't do. Pick the bad ones and they got used on him. Usually his sister would pick the good ones first, sometimes even mess up his if he had his before she did. She'd do it for fun. She'd get to the best lilies first and give them to his momma at Saturday supper. She *always* had the flowers. He always didn't. Spankings that he never understood followed supper.

Years from then, he grew angry at the thought of holding a family together with visits of flowers. He tried to think of his sister, now dead, and figure if she ever could have dreamed how he would turn out. She picked too many flowers. He got too many whippings. He had felt it. *Beat the shit out of them both . . . out of them all.* And what sense of family did he have now, years away, drunk and afraid to go into his own home? Sylvie might tell a different story. She didn't like flowers either.

There was a time when he could reason with Sister, tell her how he felt, bargain with her, whatever; it was better than now. *Goddamn idiot, sittin' on the curb in front of my own damn house.* She's *up there.* Figures passing back and forth, stopping, glancing. *She up there, the bitch, her and Sylvie, lookin' down here. I jus' know it.*

He used to be able to talk to her. That was the time Shorty had called good times or something like that. Back when he felt like his job meant he was a little larger than he was and when he thought he was in control of anything. *Hell, everything . . .*

Right around that time Sylvie got pregnant. Sister would come to help out. Folks were like that. Occasionally she did the shopping, a little cleaning (never enough to mess her hair or chip a nail) and cooked for Shorty when he got home. Shorty couldn't figure out whether it was good or bad to have two women in his house that he thought he was in control of. Of course, Sister came when she wanted and never was around when he came home angry and drunk; at least not for a while anyway. Mostly she came to drink. Along with random visits, every other Friday Shorty could count on cashing his paycheck at four and watching Sister help him drink it down at eight. Or on Thursdays, she would stroll in just after lunch, wake up Sylvie, and swing a bottle between them.

For a while things went well. Sylvie had been happy, Sister only came around once or twice a week, and Shorty would even stay home; that is, when Sister brought the booze. Now he could sigh about it: a bond of convenient companionship, cemented with quick laughs and plenty of liquor. He remembered growing to like having her around. Her company seemed comfortable. She used to make him laugh. He realized back then something he hated now: he really never knew Sylvie.

There were even a few drunken nights he remembered taking Sister to Lonnie Mack's for after-hours drinks. He never remembered exactly why he had taken her out except that he liked the way she smiled and flirted like she was his woman for a night. Or perhaps it was the way he felt, playing along with it. He smiled as he remembered trying to introduce her to the fellas and explain exactly why his wife wasn't with him.

How many wives you got, Shorty? Eddie had coughed from behind the pool table. And Shorty would never answer him. Instead he would just give Eddie a look that they both knew had to do with the woman Eddie was always huddled with in his smoke and the shadows; a woman named Patty who eventually fell into the mistake of having Eddie as a husband for four years. Sister would laugh right along with it. She smiled her it-ain't-nuthin'-but-a-thang smile and got them drinks from the bar as if she had always known the place.

Shorty supposed the "better times" had been when he could sit long hours on the back porch on Sundays and have conversations with Sister and Sylvie. Drunken afternoons, given to humid, clammy underarm heat and slurred words between sighs and whiskey ice teas. Shorty had set up the porch real nice, went out and bought three lawn chairs, and very proudly he would make the drinks. They shared the heat of the early evening, laughed over whose relatives were craziest, who might die next. Shorty could remember the folds of darkening clouds of so many nights when the liquor had loosened him enough to dream out loud. He'd talk of owning several taxis or learning to play the trombone and travel the country. Once he'd begun to tell them what he would do if he were a sculptor. He'd work hot iron and brushed aluminum around huge slabs of concrete that he'd pull right from the alley out back. He remembered Sylvie smiling warmly at this. She asked what all of that work would represent. Shorty held his drink and couldn't answer. Sister laughed out into the dark of the back yard. She hooted and said he'd have the police on his ass so soon he'd wished he'd been a locksmith instead. *Ain't room for us in that line of work, honey* . . . Sister let her deep laugh fade into the early night and Shorty watched the outline of Sylvie's silent figure sitting very still in the dark and somehow seeming smaller as a silhouette. It must have been between that time and the nights Shorty wouldn't come home (or Sister wouldn't leave) that he began to feel he was losing control of his homelife. Or was it when he started beating Sylvie? Or was it really just after Sylvie's whiskey-withered body wouldn't turn out a baby? Even now, Shorty got cloudy about all of that.

And was it supposed to be now, outside his house, that he started thinking about being a "man"? A big, strong, tall man. THE man. Thinking like that made him chuckle, even when he didn't feel like laughing. Then he smiled, the kind of smile he would get when his daddy came to mind: *hell, if you was half a man, you'd get on up in there an' tell both them wimmen what for . . .* He breathed deeply, thinking that he should do like his daddy would, but the thought wasn't enough to move him from the curb in front of his own house, afraid to face two women: one that he knew he could never overcome with mental strength and the other that he believed he was controlling with physical power.

But beating Sylvie—even touching her—he could never do driven by strength. The fear. The looks. Helpless gray in the face. And the eyes: the way they sat close together with a sharpness that was stronger than his fists. *Hate that shit so goddamn much, Sylvie, why you lookin' like that? Get that shit-look off your face! Hell, startin' to look jus' like . . .* And he was seeing *her* right there. Maybe it was the sense of Sister's eyes in Sylvie's face that made him want to hit it. . . . *swell it up, close those fuckin' eyes up!* But big men don't get that angry. Big men control their punches and keep belts from getting wrapped around fists. Big men control their outbursts and keep their temper, right? Hold it in. Big men can do this. Even when they're called Shorty.

He remembered visiting Sister's house in more pleasant times. He remembered most the whiskey drop-ins after the bar closed down, trying to explain to himself just why he was on her porch, ringing her doorbell. The fellas were constantly on him about it. Remarks about how many drinks it took him to forget about Sylvie never got through to him. He just remembered the lure, the hard fascination of this different woman that he was afraid to touch, the ease of going from the bar to a woman that he wouldn't have to worry about abusing. On more sober, clear-headed nights he would stand up at the table and yell to the fellas that there wasn't anything going on. No sex. *No nuthin'.* But the fellas were the fellas. And they had laughed about it. Even he laughed sometimes.

"Now you know Sister ain't nothin' but a lady I happen to know."

"Yeah, I *'knowed'* her, too. A lot!"

"Watch it, brother! Sister ain't never done nuthin' with you, Eddie, so stop lyin'! She ain't never wanted to neither."

"Why you so bugged-out if nothin's hap'nin 'tween you two?" Reggie had said. "Seems to me you been visitin' too much an' explainin' too damn little. And shit, why the hell you always call her 'Sister'?"

"Because I love her." Shorty had answered quickly, urgently, with the immediacy of wanting to say something before he swallowed his drink. "I love her . . ." He let the liquid drip to his chest, dribbling like a small boy gulping milk. The whiskey soaked into him. *I love her?* And the thought had hit him, sitting there getting drunker and the fellas, shocked, confused, staring at him. ". . . like a sister."

He had let it roll out and drift into the air, wanting no response. He lowered the glass to the table and focused on his feet turned inward, his hands dangling from his knees. The ring had glittered in the shadow under the table. The way it caught light was enough to make his breath a hard substance to work in and out of his body.

Even now, on a curb in the middle of the night, even when he closed his hands together, he could feel it. Years were gone and stolen away and still, he could feel it. . . . *love her like a sister* . . . He couldn't believe he had said it. He was amazed how easily, in the space of mere moments, he could admit to it. And the fellas: they just stared. *Like a . . . goddamn sister.* Shorty didn't even care what he told them now. *Things gonna git dif'rent. Right now. Ain't allow'n no more.*

It was hot. There was a sweat and a warmth that made sitting on the curb, sitting outside his house, sitting outside of his cab, *sitting in the same goddamn place, every time, anytime, all the time* . . . unbearable.

The heat of his head took to his body. The warmth and tension lit his muscles and his hands twitched with the need to break something, overpower it to the point of defeat.

There were times when he could think straight about holding onto something tight; holding onto something with strength, like nights that Sylvie and he knew nothing of bruises and booze and spitted curses. On the curb he tried to remember the last time he didn't swear at her when he came in the house. *That shit ain't my fault. She jus' need to b'have. Stop axin' that woman inta my house. Hell, ain't my fault; Sylvie bring that shit on herself.* But it was supposed to be all right to feel like that. The fellas would tell him that. He liked knowing that at least *they* would never turn on him, or at least they would never threaten him. They never threatened. They just joked around.

He thought he could see them across the street, flittering in shadows under a lamp post. The fellas, right there, right across the street. . . . *laugh niggers. Goddammit, laugh at me.* He stood up to look at the shifting shadows. *Who the fuck lookin' at me?* He stood there, reeling from the rush of blood and booze and heat to his head.

"All right, mutha fucka, make yo' goddamn move! Move, dammit!" He stepped a few feet forward, the whiskey moving him more than his desire to move, the fists clenched as if they had been waiting all night for this. "C'mon, Reggie, don't mess 'roun'. I'll beat yo ass if you messin'!"

But he knew it wasn't Reggie or the fellas. Just him and the dark shadows. The night was a companion that he could swear at and threaten. He knew it wouldn't challenge him back. The night couldn't intimidate him; he knew it would be gone soon. As he stepped into the middle of the street, the bushes made themselves less challenging, the shadows fleeing from the form his head had wanted them to have.

"Goddamn straight! Best not be no shit messin' wit' me!" Out there in the middle of the street, he looked down. His hands swung, bouncing off his thighs, unwilling to give up the fists they had worked themselves into. He became absorbed in staring at them, watching the flesh fatten around his fingers as he squeezed tighter. They were ready.

Then something moved. He spun quickly, squarely. He jerked his fists up so fast that the momentum carried him a few dizzy steps forward. He heard something. The trash cans. They seemed to spring to his eyes in the blaze of his cab's headlights. His fists led him there, shielding his anxiety. *. . . all right, goddammit, I ain't takin no more . . .* He staggered toward the cans with the weight that he believed his fists had, ready to do something. *Do something.* Movement was all that was in his mind. Get there. Break it! End it. Stop it. Cut it out. *Stop it!* But just outside the ring of blue light from above and just before the ray of headlights, he stopped. He stood there, his arms still out, fists ready. But no movement.

He lowered his arms, but still his nails dug into his palms. Fear. It wasn't a word he used often, or that he recognized clearly. He could squeeze his hands tighter and picture the face his father must have had when he realized that he could never handle a woman and her children. He could see that face as it ran. He imagined the night that his daddy ran, the night that his daddy decided that Shorty or his sister didn't need a father around getting drunk, hitting them and giving in to Momma. That was the face. The fear. Maybe that was all it ever was.

Again, he told himself why he was standing there . . . *too many goddamn dranks. I got a mind to cut inta sumthin' anyhow . . .* He looked up to the house and he could see the blue of the T.V. throwing the women's shadows across the drapes. *Yeah, go ahead, woman, I got sumthin' for you. I got a mind to tear inta sum-* A light breeze pushed a paper bag through the group of trash cans. Shorty jerked his head that way.

"Goddammit, cut that shit out!" He lunged into the headlights' rays and watched the stretched shadow of his legs lie across the dents and curves of the cans. Someone was still trying to get at him. Something moved. A can rolled to the side.

"That's it mutha-" Shorty charged the cans. "That's yo' ass!" And he attacked the cans blindly, as if the cab's lights had pushed him to it. He thrashed among the cans, flailing, punching, kicking, bruising, getting bruised. "Go 'head, talk shit now! Where the hell are you?! Say sumthin' goddammit, please give me jus' one damn reason to break your ass! Say sumthin' . . ." He continued to flail. The heat had him now. His fists were ripe for hitting, and the blood on them made their movement quicker, more urgent. "C'mon, say sumthin'. C'mon!" He moaned with every can that received his blows and he reveled in the smell and feel of it. Metal and rotten food, soiled diapers and old cat litter, blood, sweat, and stench of whiskey breath. And the heat, the anger. . . . *dammit . . . say sumthin' . . .*

And, as he thrashed, something caught his eyes. The car lights. They sliced right into him, lying there among the garbage and cans and shit and blood. He stopped. Tipping his head back, he looked up. The sky was the only thing that seemed certain all of a sudden. Shorty noticed how few stars were in the night. He liked that; nothing to concentrate on, not as many places to look at that he couldn't get to. The night suddenly was on him, as if it were a lid being lowered on his anger.

"Please say somethin' tonight . . ." he whispered, ". . . please . . . say-"

"Shorty? Shorty is that you?" Someone was blocking the light from the right headlight. "Boy, what the hell are you doing out here?"

He jerked his head up and blinked. The glare from the left light nearly blinded him, but to the right he could recognize the bright color and tight fit of the pants. It was her. Shorty let his head fall back, resting on some newspaper that smelled like sour meat. It was her. "Where's Sylvie at?" he said.

No quick response. Just the jingling of ice in a glass and quiet drunken laughter. "She's in the house."

He could feel his body wanting to tense, his hands again wanting energy to tighten, but he was tired. He opened his eyes and looked straight up into the sky. The heels came towards him slowly. From over him she came into view: the silhouette of the done-up hair, the grinning capped teeth, and long, red fingernails wrapped around a cocktail glass. He focused on her teeth.

"Mornin', Shorty dear."

Those damn teeth. It was like her mouth was the only thing on her face. Shorty closed his eyes and the grin, like a bright photograph negative, stuck to his eyelids. His stomach knotted with the knowledge that even though his eyes were closed, he could still picture her face, the teeth, and the hair bent over his pitiful self.

"Well, I s'pose them cans know best not to fool with you, now don't they, dear?" She jingled the glass and sipped on the alcohol. "What you tryin' to ketch in that mess anyhow, honey?"

For a moment, he didn't move. It wasn't fear, that's what he was trying to tell himself. He pushed the paper from his head and slicked the gritty sweat-blood mixture from his face. The blue of the street light caught the moist skin of his forearms; blue fire on the curves of his muscles and deepness, black crevasses, spreading in the creases and wrinkles. He slapped a hand to his eyes, not trusting his ability to close them. Slowly, cautiously, he slid his hand down his face and relaxed when he was sure that his eyes were closed. . . . *No more . . .* He started to run through his head what he was going to say to Sister, what he was going to do when he got up. . . . *ain't 'fraid no more, woman. Best not be in my way* . . . With his eyes closed he almost smiled, imagining how he would handle this. He lifted his head and began to get up. Then she touched his knee. He stopped moving. . . . *I ain't gonna be—I got no reason to be 'fraid.*

She bent closer, her alcohol-warm breath breezing where sweat and blood had soaked his shirt to his chest. He sighed at the feel of the chill on his skin and let the warmth of her breath take his neck. Now, he didn't feel it: the fear. It was something else. She moved her hand from his knee to the wetness of his shirt. Her breathing: he could hear the warmth of it. He could feel the weight of it. He felt the way it brushed his lips; it wasn't the sweetness, but the thickness. And like a dripping syrup, a sensation surged through the skin of his neck and tightened his chest, rippled his stomach and then dark, slow, thick, heavy breath burned below his waist.

"Where—where's Sylv . . ." A heat gripped his lungs. "Where's my wife?" His eyelids fluttered open and he shivered at the closeness of her face, her breasts, her tight pants, her teeth, still grinning.

"I thought we already been through that." She pressed down onto his chest.

"Look, Sister, don't mess around! I had enough tonight. If I'm asking for my wife, I don't need no foolin' and-" He shoved her hands away. No fear. ". . . an' jus' keep your hands on that damn glass! Your hands moving in places they jus' need to leave alone."

"I s'pose them trash cans'd have the same to say to you." She chuckled. "I ain't never seen no man so bent on makin' such a mess." Now she wasn't grinning widely, but calmly, barely smiling, almost as if she was trying to curve her lips as little as possible. He knew all about that smile, the way one side of her mouth curved towards the left dimple. He kept his eyes on it, hating it. He started to rise.

"Ain't none your bisniss what I been doing out-"

"Been drankin', aintcha?" she said. "Huh, *Shorty*?"

He shot up to his feet. "It really ain't none your god-damn biz'nis if . . ." his eyes leveling at her face, his voice leveling, too, ". . . I been drankin' or not." All the times he'd hated her, all the insults, all the times he should have told her to go home, pulsed in a knot in the front of his head. The spins from the alcohol set in slowly, sneaking up on his control. He started losing a clear vision of her. *All them times . . . Woman tryin' to hook me. Tryin' to git me.* The times that meant something to him, bad and good, spun through his head and taunted his eyesight, playing with the way her hair looked to him. Sister's hair seemed to be too much, twice its volume, lurching back and forth towards him. She had dyed it in a light color and the headlights illuminated it to a brownish, brassy fire. He could see it, that gold, swirling blaze, grabbing hold of him, bands of shiny hair wriggling around his head, his chest, shoulders, fingers. *Don't mess wit me. Stop messin'*! Her hair seemed to lunge. He just stood there. He could feel wind from somewhere cooling his chest. Sister bent down and put the glass on the asphalt.

"Like these shoes I just got?" She stayed bent long enough for him to see the flow of her spine rise and slide into the firm shape that filled her pants. She was taking off her heels. "You like these?" She had the sort of tone in her voice that Shorty would've liked his daughter to have, if he had a daughter. When she straightened up, barefoot, her eyes were level with Shorty's. And her lips: the gloss of red looked fresh. He was glad that Sylvie never wore lipstick. He clasped his hands together.

"You better just—jus' git on home, Sister." *I ain't 'fraid.*

"I'm in the middle of the street right now, dear. I ain't in your house or your yard, so don't tell me. I don't got to git home or no place if I don't want to."

"Well, you don't got to stay 'roun here." He looked to the house. She stepped closer.

"Why?" Again, warm air pushing into his skin.

He didn't look at her. He knew she was grinning that mocking grin of hers. *No fear.* He kept his eyes on the T.V. light in his house and let words fall quietly from his mouth. "Sister, don't, I—Woman, look, I got a damn big urge in me to . . ." His fingers were jerking with excitement. "Jus' don't." Fingers twitching into fists.

"What? If you can't handle this, then that's your problem, honey-chile, ain't mine. We in the middle of the street; I'm doin' what I want. I cain't help it if you never do."

He looked at her and let go a slow, evolving smile. It was one of those smiles that doesn't always mean the person was meaning to smile. She stepped back when she saw the light catch his face. In her eyes he felt the weight of his smile. He could feel the grin in his teeth, in his jaw, in the skin of his forehead. When he put his hand to his head to wipe the sweat, he barely noticed it was clenched. *Yeah, woman, I'm doin' what I want, too.* He rubbed his shirt with his palm. The sweat was coming back.

"Yeah, we *are* in the middle of the street, ain't we?" He stepped closer to her. "I ain't in my house or my yard neither. What we gonna do 'bout that?"

Catching her breath, she smoothly stepped to meet him. "I don't know, Shorty," she said. "What do you *think* we gonna do?" And she took hold of his collar, pulling at it, playing with it.

It startled him. Reacting and then controlling himself, his fist nudged her ribs, knowing how hard he could have struck. If he had.

She gasped. She knew, too. And that made her giggle.

"What's so damn funny?"

"I guess jus' watchin' you tryin' to figure out what you cain't do." She was staring straight at him.

"An' what's that?"

"You tell me, Shorty." Those eyes: cutting. "You don't even know what to do with me, do you?"

I'll tell you what I'm gonna do to—

"What, you gonna do that same thing to me as you did to them cans, dear?"

Best ease off woman, goddammit. I got a mind to cut inta sumthin' and . . . He looked down, away from her.

"You gonna beat cans again tonight, Shorty?"

He could hear her laughing, feel her tugging his collar. And then his body moved. Rigid, quick, fast, heat and sweat and hands taking over, he swung the back of his fist past her nose, knocking her hand from his collar. He grabbed her waist.

"You want me to tell you what I'm gonna do?" He

pulled her closer. "You wanna *know,* woman!" One hand moved upward and found itself balled into a fist of her hair. She didn't move. He pushed her deeper into the cab's lights until her back bumped the hood. He craned over her, pushing onto her. He pulled her tight against him, so that her breasts spread on his chest. His other hand slid around to her back and into her pants. "You gettin' an' idea now?" He pulled her head toward his face. He could see his face in her eyes. He could see his eyes. They had a look that only saw flesh. He could feel the moist, foul warmth of his breath bouncing off her face. "Say sumthin' now."

She didn't move. She stared straight into him. His eyes saw flesh, and she seemed to see it, too.

"Go on, say sumthin'. I'm waitin'. Say jus' one fuckin' thing!" His words lacked breath. *All I gotta do is stop it. Stop the goddamn messin' around. Break it! No more, no more . . .* From far off, he heard himself, "No more." He loosened.

She slowly, smoothly moved out of his grip, but didn't move from him. Her body was still pressed to his sweat and grime and blood. She even ground her hips a little, taunting. "So," she said on a breath, "*this* is how Shorty likes it."

He rose from her and sat down in front of the cab. His head was drenched in car light and he stared ahead at the distorted shape his shadow made against a can. He saw nothing on either side of him, but he could hear her pick up her shoes, put them on and walk towards her car, mumbling *crazy-ass nigger.* He finally turned just enough to see her black high heels get into the gray car. She drove off and he lowered his head. He concentrated on the pulse of pain in his head and how, like something thick, it flowed down into the rest of his body.

The fatigue of sitting there made him get up. He went to the driver's side of the car and turned out the lights. The cans disappeared, gone from the glare. Then slowly, as his eyes adjusted to the dark, they reappeared, huddled in the glint of the street lamp. He noticed Sister's half full glass of bourbon in the street. He looked to the house. The T.V. was still on, but was Sylvie still up?

Down the street he could see Miss Eula's day lilies glowing in the night. Without thinking he walked down the center line and over to the lilies. They weren't completely in bloom, but the stalks were still quite tall and the unopened buds were almost full. From where he stood he could see his house up on the left and the blue T.V. light dancing on the posts of his porch. Quickly, clumsily, he grabbed a handful of lilies and started towards the house. He caressed them and straightened them up as he walked. *Please say somethin' tonight . . . please . . .*

As he neared the house, he could see Sylvie on the porch. He stopped. At first it was only her hair that he noticed, straight, tired and brown, almost gray in the street light. She was swaying a little, cradling a bottle. She had on a dress from work, and Shorty noticed how it seemed too big on her. . . . *please* . . . He thought she was looking at him, or looking for him, but she was saying something else.

"Sister? That you? Where you gone to? *Sister?*" She leaned against the corner post with a sad sense of age and a respect for the calm of the night. Shorty waited until she went back inside, when she realized Sister had gone. . . . *please* . . . He began to walk slowly toward the house, but picking up pace. As he walked, he tore buds off the stems of the lilies. . . . *please* . . . He passed the car and started up the steps, almost at a jog. The breeze swept the petals from his hands as he tore at them. His feet were heavy on the porch and he banged the door open. From the kitchen he could hear her.

"Sister . . . ?" she repeated.

"*Goddammit!*" He ran toward the kitchen, hands clenched around the stems. He turned the corner.

And there she was: his wife, right in his face.

"Oh, it's you." She stood there, so quietly, work dress still on, and quite comfortable in the frame of the door. He noticed the traces of smudged lipstick on the bottle she held. Her lips were carelessly, awkwardly red.

"Dammit, Sylvie." He squeezed the stems harder.

She looked down and saw the damaged, wilted lily stems, one bud still left dangling. She looked up into his eyes and he knew what she was thinking.

"Just let me take off my dress," she said quietly. "It's new." She put the bottle down and walked towards the bathroom. The alcohol had done nothing to loosen the weariness from the way she moved.

When she closed the door behind her, Shorty realized that his hand had let go of the stems. He bent down and gathered a few of them from the floor, but stopped; he could find no reason to retrieve all of them now. He stood and walked out the front door. The front porch seemed calm in the darkness. He sat down on the steps and fumbled the remaining lily stems through his hands. He could hear Sylvie come out of the bathroom and he knew that she had changed into her robe.

Other People's
Houses

*T*he house wasn't all that large or challenging. That was good for a starting place. It looked loose, easy. I remember standing on the beach one day with Tyler and Jack, looking at it, sizing it up like it was some homely girl we were flipping a coin over. Somehow Tyler convinced us that these people were wasting valuable resources by spending only a few months a year in their Cape houses. Back then, Tyler was new to the restaurant where we all worked, and he knew that winter-time tips on Cape Cod didn't easily pay the rent. It was his idea to "do" a house. Even through all of the rationalizing, even after it had happened and I was there, in somebody else's bedroom, I could not figure out why we had done it so easily.

"You've got the crowbar, right? This one needs a crowbar," Tyler had said as we began.

"Sure, Tyler." Jack's voice was heavy.

"Now, Rich, here, take this and pry slowly. Can't pull any wood out . . ." Tyler was sweating. "No! Watch it! Use the flashli- dammit! Gwen!" Tyler's eyes were wide with excitement as he scanned the dark for the fourth of our breaking-and-entering quartet.

"What?!" Gwen was startled. She was sitting back on her heels, working on a third cigarette. She didn't care that Tyler had told her not to smoke. The cigarette tip was a small point of angry light in the dark and when she inhaled, it glowed more fiercely, as if it should have made a sound. For the brief moment that she held the smoke in, the cigarette tip lit up the strands of blond hair framing her face, and in that quick flash of a moment I could see her eyes looking at me from behind that hair. She was trying not to look scared.

"Get the goddamn light over here," Tyler said.

"I don't see why we couldn't just use their hidden key that you found," she said.

"They'd know somebody had been in the house, Gwen," Tyler said.

"Oh, and pulling their back door off won't give it away? I can see them now: 'oooh, honey, what's that draft? Oh, dear, I think I left the sun porch door open last year . . .'"

"Shut up. Just point the damn light!"

I was sweating. As I pried, the lock housing gave way like a spoon pulled from thick frosting. No loud creak. Just a dry, submissive sliding.

"Damn if this place doesn't want us," Jack rasped almost as if he were coughing. I could smell the Schlitz beer on the mist from his mouth. The smell lingered long enough for me to feel sick. But then the door quietly gave way.

We were in. Much like my other first times—drinking, having sex, or taking the SATs—doing the first house wasn't very dramatic or eventful. The dance was over and the next morning found us tired, drinking someone else's coffee, not saying anything as each of us silently tried to dismiss the bad in our arrival.

Breaking into this house had its risks, but we had worked out the justifications. It was too small and bland for anyone to care that we would use it for a while. Besides, we meant no harm. That made us feel more whole, at least until the next house. Within a month we were seasoned and calloused. By the time the early days of March came, we had finally solved the grayness of winter Cape Cod life by delving into the intrigue, challenge and hedonism of breaking into other people's houses.

It was remarkable to watch us then, driving from yard to yard looking for a certain seductiveness in a house. I could feel the remorse rolling away from us as every possible conquest came into view. Perhaps the hidden value we place in all rare or taboo things becomes a little less rich when we discover how easily we can exploit them without remorse. I can remember thinking that so clearly one night in the car as we "house hunted," but I held it in, feeling suddenly inappropriate and embarrassed by my thoughtfulness.

I was always *just arriving,* always *just moving in.* That, I told myself, made it seem less of a wrong thing. If I'm moving in, if I'm in the process of walking through that door or crawling through that window, I haven't really done it. The house hasn't been violated *yet.* I just couldn't look back and condemn myself for what I hadn't done yet. Present tense came to be my redeemer. I'm *doing* it, not *done* it.

That's what got me through the stress when I found myself in the first house. I had already been upstairs and had put my bag in the room that I felt would be best for me. It was a small room, maybe a child's or a spare for an aunt that might visit during July. The wallpaper was old but still respectable, sailing schooners and sloops on a sea of off-white. The quilt on the bed was also old but its frayed corners looked well-loved. I sat on the bed for a moment, testing its bounce and I suddenly caught a glance of myself in the mirror on the closet door, which was slightly ajar. My skin, stark and bold against the pale wallpaper, seemed a deeper brown than I had ever seen it.

I got up from the bed quickly and stepped to the mirror from an off angle, so that I couldn't watch myself move in this strange, anonymous room. Just before I closed the door, I looked inside the closet. I opened it only a little, and the light entered enough for me to see the stacks of monogrammed blankets, a few shirts hanging, a pile of framed photographs, an old formless straw hat, a doll with one arm gone. More than breaking in, more than sitting on the bed or realizing that a Black person had probably never been in that house before, those items made me feel what I was doing. I was afraid to put my bag on the bed. Who had slept there before me? I set the bag next to the door and slept on a couch in the study for three nights.

I was just trying this thing out, I told myself, even whispering it, as if hearing myself speak made it real. But the next morning I kept anticipating the use of things in the house. Soon I'd have to open the cupboard and use those plates or pull a stranger's quilt from a cedar chest to keep myself warm. *So this is really me,* I thought, *this is me violating, no, using, somebody's home.* No, *house.* Summer house with a lower case "h." I had to remind myself of that. And in sparks and flashes, my guilt was almost present long enough to make me tremble then. But that was the first house.

· · · · ·

A house had to *speak* to you, Tyler had instructed us. It had to show its affluence, its overbearing waste of airspace on our planet, its need to be shared with the proletariat, and any other bullshit he could attach. He was an N.Y.U. dropout who had read too much leftist literature to ever live comfortably with himself, but with his use of language—rich bilingual allusions and an elusive but attractive vocabulary—

he just sidestepped the appearance of being obnoxious. He seemed so *genuine*, harmless even, such a Robin Hood quality to his voice. He effortlessly won us over. It wasn't hard. When you lived on the Cape for the winter, you claimed it as your own. So many of the summer residents seemed to leave it easily, like perfectly good shoes not to be used for a long time. And what was to be done with all of this unused and neglected space? It *wasn't* wrong to use what the rich neglected. Tyler had delivered that doctrine like poetry and suddenly we didn't feel as if we were really contemplating a crime. The idea seemed to come to each of us like the thought of a useful invention. Serendipitous, Tyler called it.

Jack caught on early in the search for houses to be lived in. Jack didn't care one way or another about much of anything. He put his efforts into drinking, learning pick-up lines and not exercising. If she had had it in her to be knowingly blunt, Gwenneth, who had just begun to tag along with us, might call someone like Jack a slug. Gwenneth already had a place she could live in without having to risk the chance of spending the winter in the Hyannis jailhouse, but she was tragically nineteen and bored with life. Her parents, back in Shaker Heights, thought she was at Kenyon, studying art.

Tyler might have described Jack more colorfully, passing him off as being something like *invidious*. But Tyler liked Jack; they thought alike sometimes, the way hawks and maggots, regardless of nature's hierarchy, both depend upon meat for sustenance. They were our guides by association, hunters and collectors of homes. But I really can't sound too indicting. I mean, where did I fit in?

My father said I was lost. If I'd ever asked him, he would tell me that I didn't fit in. I had run the full course of the New England college routine and I had enough oxford shirts and wool socks to possess the *feel* of Cape Cod. But you just don't run into many Black males, L. L. Bean sweater or not, on the dunes of the Cape. He knew. He had been in and out of these houses for years. Barbecues, teas, company parties. All functions for the bank and his bosses. I had heard all about them. Now I could only see those houses through his bitterness.

When I told him that I was going to spend the winter on the Cape, he told me to be careful. *Not many Black folks out there,* he said, *except as maids. Not many of them period.* I laughed and told him he was being ridiculous. He *didn't* laugh back and told me to stay in touch.

One night, sitting in that first house, I called my father. I wanted to tell him where I was. On the fourth ring, I realized that I didn't know whose house I was in. It was like remembering only the eyes or backside, not the name, of a person in bed next to you the day after some drunken party.

Then he answered. I listened for a few moments, him asking several times who it was. I remember hearing a soft scraping sound over the line and thinking that that must have been my father's whiskers brushing the phone, and I thought as I hung up how, for all the years before he retired, his face always seemed to be clean shaven, even at night.

· · · · ·

"Why should *my* mind be troubled by it," Jack said, "as long as there isn't an alarm system and nothing too valuable is missing, I don't have any goddamn troubles."

"But, I mean, isn't there something about morals that's missing?" Gwenneth asked.

"Morals stay on the mainland and folks come out here to get rid of them. The *suits* have to dump their baggage. They let it fly on the Canal Bridge and by the time they get here: hell, lock up your wife and pets!" Jack said "suits" as if his distaste warded off the idea that he might be one someday.

Gwenneth frowned. "That's idiotic—'leave morals on the mainland . . .'" She was at times too thoughtful for the life that contained her. She made jewelry and was forever leafing through 20-year-old issues of *The New Yorker* that she kept in her car, giggling at cartoons and Saks Fifth Avenue ads. Things should have been that simple some of the time, she felt. "You use morals all the time." She was sprawled out on a futon couch among large pillows.

From the bar joining the kitchen to the dining and living rooms, I watched her ruffle through old Sunday editions of the *Boston Globe*. I was cooking and I would look up when I felt that she might not notice me staring at the way she lay half visible on the futon, the stretch of her hip and thigh matching the soft, inviting curve of the pillows which surrounded her.

Jack laughed, crushing ice savagely in his mouth. His teeth were yellow from smoking Pall Malls with the filter broken off. The last house we hit had five cartons stashed under the pantry sink. They were wrapped tightly in dark plastic. He seemed overjoyed that he not only got free cigarettes, but that they were concealed in brown plastic, as if he had unearthed someone's secret stash.

Jack spit a huge chunk of ice at the fireplace. "When you get to a certain point, Gwen, you use what you want."

"Or when you can't do that, use other peoples'. Isn't that right, Jack?" I yelled from the kitchen.

Tyler only mumbled from his half sleep on the other couch.

"But wait . . ." Gwenneth let her hair fall in front of her face. This usually made the smart boys tell her everything. "How do you *leave* your morals? And what is it that you 'use'?"

"Gwenneth, it's not like your goddamn kidneys. I'm just saying that morals you can forget about when it's convenient; throw them away and use whatever else you have to get what you want."

Tyler stirred from his blanket of newspapers. "Gwen, dear, Jack is saying that morals are easily cast aside for your sanitary pleasure."

Gwenneth let one of her eyes be seen from her veil of hair. The eye wasn't satisfied. "What in the hell do you mean?"

"Morals are like underwear," I said.

"Right." She was baffled.

"When they get too tight, too clammy, too hot or when we shit in them, we just put on a new pair that feels more comfortable."

"Oh right, yes, yes! Good thought, Rich!" Tyler eagerly folded the paper. "Don't give an unemployed English major idle time. He'll browbeat you with figures of speech! Ha!"

"Underwear . . . that's good." Jack laughed. "Wonder how many pair I've put on this year."

"Just one," I said. "You don't mind the shit that builds up in them."

"What do your dirty BVDs have to do with morals?"

"Gwen, wise up." Jack didn't like how this was going. "It's called figurative language. The bright fellows are getting hard-ons. Morals are like underwear. It's a goddamn metaphor, or simile. Something like that."

"Why can't you guys just talk about it clearly instead of using spiced-up bullshit words to avoid the real deal?"

"Because we're goddamn bored!" I said. "When you don't have something that's real and tangible, you have to add color to your life in some way. You must figure out a way to spice up your life or you die."

"And so *morals* aren't real?"

"Ask Jack," Tyler smiled.

"Jack?"

"Fuck morals."

Gwenneth sat up. "But you still haven't told me what you really think of morals."

"What do *you* think of morals, Gwenneth?" Tyler said.

Gwenneth said nothing. She raked her hair away from her face several times. She had grown into the habit of doing this when her mind was troubled. Someone must have taught her that a girl with hair in her hands was in need of attention. She said nothing but cast her hair from her face one last time and, as it fell, it flashed brilliantly, angrily against the deep burgundy fabric of the futon. Even buried in so many pillows, she suddenly looked uncomfortable. The room was very silent for a while, with only the gurgle of water boiling on the stove and hint of wind blowing through the gable above where the summer occupants of the house had forgotten to close the eaves vent.

· · · · ·

The second house was a modest gem. Smallness was important. If it was small, there was less to ruin, less to take, less to consider abusing. Jack liked the remoteness of the place; lost in folds of gray trees several hundred yards from the main road. Gwenneth thought the blue trim on gray wood was cute. I laughed at that as Jack punched in a pane of the sun room window. That's what she said: cute. I could imagine the group she must have hung out with at Kenyon. They were probably still sitting in some basement, stoned, wondering when Gwenneth was going to show up with the pizza.

But it was a nice house: hardwood floors, new carpet, a bar that was stocked for a nuclear fallout and a freezer filled with Weight-Watcher's meals. Free meals were always a good thing. There was even a fold-out couch. Perks of the trade.

When Tyler moved in his crate of books, he sighed with contentment. He tapped the door plaque that read *Welcome to the Fitzsimmons'* and said, "Honey, we're home."

We had picked that one well. Jack even bought a case of beer to celebrate the good find. Funny, that; we celebrated. In some twisted way, now that I think about it, we would have made great real estate agents.

· · · · ·

Perhaps at times I *was* lost. To see me with them, there on the Cape, I looked out of place. One Black kid with three sardonic White kids. But in my mind, at the core of my heart, I often felt as if I were the most *appropriate* of our group. There was that sense of perpetually just having arrived that I held onto. But I had come to live on the Cape not trying to fit into it. On my smarter days I knew that would never happen. But I yearned for it. Tyler knew this. During late nights of drinking, he would kid me.

"Richard, you may have the clothes of a benevolent visitor, but your eyes have the narrowed look of *avaricious* resolve in them." Tyler's vocabulary always made his observations seem less insulting or more insightful.

"With words like that, Tyler, I'd have to say you've been reading too much Marx."

"Richard, maybe you haven't read enough."

I always felt smaller when he called me Richard instead of Rich.

But Gwenneth was different. I told myself that I had purpose, but she didn't fool herself with that. Sometimes I mocked my own aimlessness as I tried to make Gwenneth into some waif that I could better justify knowing if she seemed less sure of herself than me. But I could hear my father's voice, perhaps just his sigh, on my nights off when I went to see Gwenneth working at the bar. I imagined his disdain for the scene: me, there on the Cape of all places, drinking in a bar and drooling over some White girl. That's how he'd put it: drooling.

In the same way that I surprised myself by standing in the front hall of someone's house that I had never known, I found it odd and inexplicable that I was at the bar more and more on my off times.

"Why do you come down here every Friday night?" she asked me sometime in mid-March. "Shouldn't you be out on the town, wooing women or drink or wooing whatever it is that you woo on a Friday night?"

"I think you've forgotten how *exciting* the Cape is during the winter, what with the dozens of discos, cathouses, nightclubs . . . It's nonstop hedonism."

"There *are* things to do. Tyler always finds things. And Jack . . ."

"Well yeah, you're right. But the *magnificent* Ambersons canceled their weenie-roast, so here I am."

"So I'm just sloppy seconds."

"Definitely sloppy. How much rum did you put in this anyway?"

"I appreciate the affection. You said rum and Coke, so you got RUM and Coke. If you wanted COKE and rum, you could have asked for it. That's the way it works."

"So when did you stop being Dean Martin's cocktail waitress?"

"When he stopped coming in here on Friday nights." She smiled, turned toward the bar, and walked away.

A few minutes later, she came back to my table with another drink for me. She sat down. "Who's Dean Martin?"

"Just a guy."

"A guy?"

"Yeah, he doesn't have breasts."

"What kind of guy is he?" She sipped from one of my drinks and winced. "Dean Martin: hmm, sounds like a car salesman."

"He's just a guy. Wears suits, drinks a lot, woos women, gets old, just like the rest of us."

"He's not like *you*, though, is he, this Dave Martin guy?" Her hair was falling into her face, but she looked playful. She let it. Her hand moved slowly, repeatedly moving it back as it fell to her cheek again.

"*Dean* Martin. No, I guess I'm not much like Dean. Not enough suits."

"Funny, funny. I'm sure you look just fine in your *suit*." She smiled and patted my cheek. "So this Martin character; is he like Jack?"

"Well, maybe so, in a way. Not as heavy. Dean is close to Jack in a twisted way but . . . ah, more hair, more mousse, more martinis."

"But they are kind of alike. I bet they'd be friends."

"More like lovers. Of course they'd always be having tiffs over who was the dominant one."

"Right. Rich, if you didn't try to be so funny all of the time, you'd be quite an ass. Damn! This drink should have a warning label on it."

"Told you. Do you always drink when you work or is it just me and my unsettling charm?"

"Yes." She took another sip and waved off my teasing. "I suppose this Dean Martian guy isn't too much like Tyler."

"The guy's name is DEAN MAR - TIN, Gwenneth."

"Oh pooh, I heard you. It's just funnier to screw with names. So is this Don Martoni guy like Tyler? I don't think anybody's close to being like him."

"Tyler *is* a strange egg to figure out."

"He sure is funny. God, he makes me laugh!"

"Do you like him?"

"What?"

"Women always admire humor in people they like. They never say it outright, but it's true."

She looked at me like I was an idiot.

"I think I heard that one on the Oprah show."

"Well, I have tried to get to know him, but he's just sort of out there, y'now?"

"Do you ever talk to him?"

"Yes, but he's always so hard to talk to around people."

"But you don't have a problem in private, do you?" I grinned. "He's a pretty *personable* guy, isn't he?"

"What?!"

"Gwenneth, *Gwenneth*, dear. It's not hard to figure out what happened the other night when Jack and I went out."

"You're joking."

"How was it?"

"No, you're sick."

"How many times?"

"Four."

I downed my drink. The alcohol curled my lips into a bitter grin. I don't think I wanted to hear that. I've always hated the importance of numbers. Four. Damn. Maybe *one* would have been all right. That might have meant drunken lust or boredom. *Two* maybe: to improve upon the first time. But *four*. And in one night. Damn.

"You really are an ass sometimes." But she was smiling, as if it was better that I knew, and now that I knew, it was all right.

"So now we're back to the original question. Do you like him?"

"It was sex, Rich. Is *liking* him really an issue?"

"I would say it isn't, but most women don't try to find out more about guys they've fucked by comparing them to Dean Martin."

"When is sex ever going to stop being such a *big* thing?"

"When kids stop liking candy. The shuga's jus' too fine darlin'! So, what makes you so *ideal* all of a sudden?"

"Hey, I'm not a slut."

"Nobody's calling you one."

"I just want to know *some*thing about Tyler. If he doesn't want to deal with me, that's all right. It helps to know a little about somebody that you've had-"

"Fucked."

The word bothered her.

"It's not like that," she said.

I wanted to say it again.

"So just help me out. What is Tyler like, I mean who could you compare him to?"

I took a gulp from the second drink. "Maybe if Cyrano De Bergerac and one of the female Cosmonauts had a kid, you'd have Tyler."

"Who and who?"

"Skip it. They're bowling partners of Dean Martin's."

Many times I imagined showing my father a picture of Gwenneth. He might have admired her breasts, but he would never allow my liking one of "those types of girls." My mother, resigned only to speak as a second motion to my father, might ask *why blond hair, Richard, why so pale?* I couldn't deal with the image of my parents' faces had I ever told them about her. How could I be sure? I didn't even know if I was *drooling*. I never had a picture of her. But it was just the picture I didn't have— the image of what I didn't own—that intrigued me.

My father could easily tell me how I didn't belong. He had worked at his bank job for twenty years to learn how little he would fit in, even if he bought the biggest house on the Cape. My father would say there were some places, some situations in which Black folks should never try to place themselves. At times I think he held back from saying how he felt because he thought I wouldn't respect him. I'd find myself at the bar some nights, staring at Gwenneth, wondering just who I *did* respect.

· · · · ·

It is amazing how doing a house is so much like what guys think getting a woman into bed is all about. First, you see only object, nothing more. You see what you want. You run over the possibilities in your mind. Alcohol softens reservations and makes it/her seem more inviting, as if she/it were signaling, *Come on, boys, try to get inside me.* You study it. You case it out, telling yourself you're rational. Like some drunk frat boy, you tell yourself *we're all adults here.* At the same time, you calculate the effort it will take, the risk involved, the consequences. You're horny, but you're trying to be rational. But how do you think rationally when you want to fuck somebody? When you want inside somebody's house?

There was that time we stood outside a house for two hours, casing it, deciding whether or not it was right. Tyler was hesitating. The house stood there, silent. Where was Errol Flynn now? I had told Tyler that my father knew who summered there. Gwenneth laughed out loud at that: *summered.*

Tyler wasn't laughing. He got tense, peering through the windows, saying it was too lavish for us. It wasn't time to make our move on this one, he felt. I told him my father worked for them and didn't like the rich bastards. The house waited innocently. It had white carpets. Jack was smiling. I told them I didn't care. Inside, I wasn't sure. I felt like an initiate trying to prove himself to a gang in some bad B-movie.

"This goddamned place is so ripe! It's so hot," Jack whispered heavily. He was wearing a balaclava, looking like an idiot.

Tyler kept on pacing, smoking. He had a used paperback of Trotsky writings that he kept twisting. I remember Tyler whispering into the night, *this is just fucked; we are fucked.* I think our readiness frightened him.

· · · · ·

"So, Rich, would you do it?" Jack asked from the back of the stockroom.

"The house in Hyannis? I'd rip 'er right open!" I was with Jack now. The lifeless chill of the stockroom felt fitting right then. Our hours together had worn an easily found groove in my character. It was all about spontaneous, thick-skinned bluntness and often vulgarity. At times I got the same feeling having conversations with Tyler. I just felt more intelligent then. "Yeah, Jack, we've got to do it. It's waiting for us." I could hear my inflated self speaking as if the real me were huddled behind stacks of beer cases, eavesdropping.

"No man, I mean *her.*" Jack stopped lifting cases.

"What?"

"Goddamned Gwenneth. Would you, y'know, take her down."

"Well . . ." My voice behind those beer cases was straining.

"I mean she *does* look hot."

I was stunned. "No. I mean, no, I wouldn't. She's not all that with it upstairs."

"Yeah, like you'd want to discuss the finer points of Camus while the bedsprings are squeaking."

"I just mean, there's got to be something more." I put all my energy and focus into moving the beer cases. I looked up at Jack when I felt that he might not be staring at me.

"Is that why you come to the bar every Friday?" He was grinning. "I've noticed; I'm not the stumbling drunk you think I am."

I tried for a light tone. "Yes, Jack, you *are* the stumbling drunk I think you are." But that was just a sandbag defense. I felt exposed, indicted. When a window is broken, a padlock pried, what can you say, standing there, crowbar in hand? He grinned at me until I had to show I noticed.

"Well, Jack, you've got me pegged dead right. *All* I think about is screwing Gwenneth's brains out." I began stacking cases again.

"Lighten up, Rich, I was just checking." He leaned against a stack of cases.

"Checking on what?"

"To see if you wanted her."

"Why?"

He stacked a case. "Why the hell do you think?"

"Well, why ask me?"

"It looked like you were into her quite a bit, man. I didn't want to step on toes."

"Jack, this isn't the Middle Ages. I don't own Gwenneth, even if I did like her."

Jack went to the beer cooler and took out two beers for us.

"Don't believe what you hear," he said, mocking drunkenness and toasting himself. We sat down and drank our beers slowly, more as something to do, rather than trying to get drunk. I smiled as I realized it was the first time I had ever witnessed Jack express any sort of care, no matter how stilted, towards anyone.

"So you have a little something for Gwen?" I sounded like a psychologist.

"I suppose I do in a way." Jack said. "Not much. I mean, I'm not looking for a girl friend. Not yet anyway."

"So what are you looking for?"

"You really are stupid sometimes."

"So all you want to do is have sex, right? That's it?"

"Well, hey man, she's the one who always looks like she's wanting it."

"What?" I began to suck at my beer heavily, wanting to be done.

"Let's just say she's come on to me and I'm going to follow up."

I was silent. They had probably been drinking. Jack had probably made some jokes. She had laughed. Maybe she touched his sleeve . . .

"We were drunk one night after work and she kept talking about taking a walk on the beach. Y'know, she wanted to be out there with me."

"And?"

"Well, we did."

"Had sex on the beach in the middle of winter?"

"No, we walked on the beach. But it was cold and she kept on grabbing me."

"No, shit, Jack, it's cold out there. I'd probably grab you too."

"It wasn't the same thing."

I finished my beer, got up, and started stacking cases again.

"So you *do* like her," Jack said, still sitting.

"Jack, use your head. No, use your goddamn eyes. Look at me . . . What do you think would happen if Gwenneth and I just happened to be frolicking in the dunes and a bunch of salty, crazy-ass Massachusetts fishermen came strolling by? I like my ass too much in one piece to get messed up with Gwenneth. Even if I did, man, it'd be a little different." I stood in the middle of the stockroom gripping an empty beer bottle. "It wouldn't be just about getting drunk and fucking. You just want her so you can say you *did* her, right? Shit. I mean, you don't just *use* people!"

"Like houses?"

I went back to stacking beer cases.

. . . . .

After so many houses, there was no more arriving to be done. Only coming and going. And an easy house lost its excitement too soon. After the fourth house, we realized we had to go for a big one. The challenge, the size, the possibility of hidden, vast, frozen-dinner cellars.

I had a dream in which my father came to me. He had just put on a linen suit picked from the closet of the man he worked for at the bank. It was the job he toiled in before he retired to his lounge chair and cable T.V. In my dream my father enjoyed my domination of the homes. He had me seated in an easy chair bolted in the middle of a Hyannis back road, and I was watching him run frantically from house to house. He had brightly colored real estate company signs tucked under his arm and he was screaming, declaring them all to be his. I cringed as he darted back to me, grinning and whispering to me *someday, son, this will all be yours.*

That night I told Tyler about my dream. He laughed. We sat on the floor of a dark living room and he laughed at me. But in the stillness, the dust and silence of a house that we had invaded, I realized *I've got to move.*

"You know, sometimes Jack thinks you're crazy," Tyler told me.

I could feel the stillness of the winter and the suspension of having no place to name as clear, or safe, or mine. "I'm just tired of the smallness. And it's not just the houses."

He laughed at that, too. He said I was missing the point. But I was committed.

• • • • •

The last house was one that my father had known. He'd been inside of it several times. The house had a nameplate hanging from the mailbox. *The Holmans.* I had been there before, too. Was I just arriving again? I tried that one as I stood in this new foyer, expecting the same detachment. But I knew that wouldn't work; I had been in *this* house. I remembered the formidable size of it from when my father brought me here with my mother; I was much younger then and, along with the house's uncomfortable size, I sensed my father's bitterness. But now I felt I could breathe in this place: we, I, had conquered the big house.

This "summer home," someone's second house, far outshone what my parents had lived in all year round as their only home. I remember how much my father had hated entering this house, the *summer* house of his boss, Hale Holman of Holman, Dwight and Holman Investors. I remember him getting dressed for the company picnics, always swearing that he'd never go to another.

For this one Jack took the lead, after my pushing, and simply found the hidden key. He did it alone. It took him a night of drunken prowling. Deep inside, I don't think he minded it, as if his was a species that consumes alcohol, copulates brutally, and provides for its offspring by foraging for Hide-a-Key cases on the backsides of drainpipes.

Tyler was disdainful of using the front door. Jack said he didn't give a shit if anyone knew he was there or how he entered. I, in my wanting, really couldn't argue. The violation was the thing, like it or not. Method no longer mattered.

Upon entering the house, setting our few bags on the floor and opening up the housewarming case of beer, Jack poured the first one directly into the seat of a leather wing chair next to the pink marble fireplace. I stiffened.

"You need to take a crap, Rich?" Jack took out another beer. "You look sick."

"Why the beer in the goddamn chair?" I tried to sound more judgmental than protective.

He stared at me and it was then that I saw him for real. His stare put a hook in me. For all of the smallness that I had believed him to be made of, Jack was a predator. More so than me, he handled this game of domination well. I thought I was the dominator, but I knew this house, its people. He rotated his body in a lazy, careless turn, letting his bitter gaze coat the room.

"Goddamn suits. Fuck 'em." He threw his half empty can into the dining room. Something broke there. I sat down holding my unopened beer. It was Tyler's turn to smile. Gwenneth was thumbing through large art books on the coffee table, already moved in.

I drank quickly, feeling alone, feeling suddenly very much a Black person in this room. I felt that sense of manners and reserved protocol that my parents had told me to have when in the presence of White people. The thought of my father came to me again: him working as a banker for people like Hale Holman whose widow now owned the house that we stood in. I tried to plan my dream that night. In it, my father would be pleased that I was dominating a realm that he could only help someone else own. And I laughed at myself the whole afternoon. Gwenneth said I was so much fun when I got drunk and lost a sense of myself.

This wasn't a cute house. It was regal, lavish, unnecessary. Calling those words to mind made me forget that I knew who the owner was. To ease myself, I explored the whole house. Walking through the place gave me a clouded sense of victory, as if I had taken some medieval castle without a single casualty. It's expense—the house and the risk of breaking in—became a necessary fulfillment.

For a brief while I enjoyed it. I remember standing in the library, listening to Jack throwing bowls and plates; I smiled. Sometime during the early evening, in the study, I bumped into Tyler prying open a locked wooden box. Moments later we were puffing on cigars; two happy bastard fathers. Tyler drifted from the study into the master bathroom with several back issues of *The Atlantic* and a bottle of vodka. I knew he would be there for hours. I watched him stroll upstairs and thought how difficult it was to believe it was me, here, allowing this. *So, this is me . . .* I walked back into the living room and then the dining room, then the kitchen, the study, the bathroom, the living room again. I wanted to find a place to sit comfortably. By my fifth trip to the kitchen, I managed to use a glass for water; I put ice in it the next time through. From the dining room bay window, I watched the tufts of withered dune grass sway on the darkening beachfront.

The evening found Jack still drinking in the kitchen. Tyler was passed out in the master bedroom. Gwenneth had found me in the dining room and together we wandered into the study. We collapsed into huge chairs and rummaged through photo albums.

Gwenneth was enveloped in quilts on a small couch, her hair flowing down. I imagined that hair moving wildly in response to Jack's thrusting movements or even Tyler's. I could see myself in the picture, but always at the window, or as the sheet that has been kicked off the bed.

I stared at her for so long that her face became unfocused. She looked up at me, saw me assessing her. She smiled. I realized how uncomfortable my chair felt.

"Look at this one, Rich." She stretched to hand me a picture she had taken out of an album. "All those kids. They're cute in a funny looking way."

I took it. It was one of those pictures that came out of the seventies: strange faded colors, washed out images, and the look on the peoples' smiling faces that made them appear sorry plaid had been so popular. Strange that someone would look so happy and yet uneasy. I said this to Gwenneth and she laughed. She said something about not always realizing what you have until you have it and I smiled, but she hadn't said it well and I wasn't really listening.

I turned back to the picture and stared at it for a long time, much in the same way I had looked at Gwenneth. The colors slid around in my vision until there were only faces. Three adult faces. Several small, round children's faces. And a house, looming, framing them more convincingly than the yellowish-white frame of the photograph paper. I began to see how much I could not fit into that picture, in my hand or in that study. And it made me angry all over again. Gwenneth was waving pictures in my face, smiling, talking. I wasn't listening.

"Let's go outside," I said. I felt my purpose fulfilling itself; it was just a matter of the way the minutes stacked up now. "I want to go outside." Gwenneth grinned at my idea. I grinned, too. The minutes were stacking and I felt justified. I headed for the door as Gwenneth fumbled with her shoes.

It was cold on the back patio. I broke into a run towards the edge of the lawn and looked down stairs that sunk into the sand of the beach. The stairs, the beach, the wood, grass; together they drifted out of steel-gray mist, pulsing in and out of the night haze and frost. I glanced back. Gwenneth came stumbling toward me, carrying a flashlight. Its rays bounced from the dune grass to the mist in the air that swirled in from the sea and back onto the house.

"Richard!"

I turned to meet her. Her voice had sounded nervous, but she jogged up to me smiling. She never called me Richard.

"There are warmer places we could go," she said, putting her arms inside my sweater. "You *are* sick, you know that?"

It was cold and she was holding me. What I felt was her hair. It blew around me, tickling my face. She held me, waiting. I looked out at the cold of the beach. I could feel her hair and it felt coarse now. It felt blonde. Like the house, it felt like something I should not be touching.

"You know, Jack tried this move on me." She massaged my back. "Nice thought, guys. But damn, it's cold out here!"

I tried to turn away from her and to the water. She shuffled with me, the flashlight ray lurching out and back on the folds of shore fog. I tried turning again. The dim light from the windows met my face.

"We look like two stiff-legged waltzers at a lawn party," she whispered and hugged me tighter. She smiled and I thought to myself, this is a harmless, gentle person. And she kept on smiling. Even here. Even now. She was always smiling.

I stiffened and asked her for the flashlight.

"Richard, I'm cold." And she held me.

I looked at the house. And I felt her hands. On my back. In my back pockets. I pointed the flashlight back at the house. Its stark paleness jumped out of the night. I pushed Gwenneth back and she stumbled into the flashlight beam. She stood there, within the outline of the house.

The house. A series of white, triangular gables. A trim of brown. Maybe it had been blue years before. An iron weather vane on the point of the largest gables. No longer there. It used to be a sailboat. Then I saw her and the house again. The woman and this big, large, unnecessary house. No, it was a *home*. A home. And it was Gwenneth standing there in front of it.

"There used to be a weather vane," I said.

"Maybe Jack's torn it off." She laughed. She stepped towards me. "Let's go inside and do this."

"No. Years ago . . . It was there. When I was a kid. I wanted to take it home. A goddamn sailboat weather vane."

She looked at the house. "Stop messing around, Rich."

"The Holmans live here."

"You *know* these people?"

I started back to the house calling for Jack and Tyler.

"Rich, this is way too strange!" she yelled.

"We've got to leave." I said. I walked to the door and looked back.

Gwenneth stayed outside for a few moments. Perhaps she was waiting, hoping that I was making all of this up. I looked at her on the lawn, set against that gray beach. She and the house seemed to be placed safely now, far from being used up.

By morning I had managed to get Tyler and Jack up and out of the house. Even though they were packed and the doors to Gwenneth's car were open, they seemed uncertain of their departure. What were they to do? I gave them some of the money I had left to make up for the sudden change in plans.

"What the hell, Rich?" Jack had a pasty crust along his lips. He was slightly hungover and slightly upset, but seemed amused at me, too.

"It's just wrong, what we're doing here," I said.

"Since when?" Tyler had already found a place in Gwenneth's car. "Where did that psychotic home-raiding lust go?" He wasn't laughing, though.

I faced them, but didn't feel like explaining. "I just can't do this, all right?" I told myself that I was above them. But all I could feel was the dirt and gravel through my pants as I sat on the front steps. I didn't even help them put their bags in the car. I didn't want to touch them.

Gwenneth was the last out of the house. She stood there, confused, her head down and hair hanging without order. She seemed worn. Maybe even older looking. Maybe just worn. She looked like she needed to be held. But I felt heavy and my clothes were dirty. They drove off, waving goodbye to me like we'd all come back next year and do the same thing all over again. I sat there, still feeling, as I had all night long while cleaning the house, that I had too many clothes on. I watched the car until trees blocked my view. I didn't know if I would be back at the bar; I didn't tell them one way or another.

I turned to the Holman's summer home, caught in hazy morning light. The home appeared smaller and less challenging to me now. It looked less brilliantly white. It was an off-white house really, but in the random flashes of sunlight, it just looked dirty. I didn't tell Mrs. Holman that when

I called her a while earlier. I didn't tell her that we were all college graduates and from good-natured families. I didn't tell her that we had thought this whole thing out and that we were questioning what we believed in every day. I didn't even tell her I was sorry. I told her that we had broken into her home. When she asked what sort of shape the house was in, I just said it was fine. Fine. I was silent until she hung up.

I walked inside, made some coffee, and sat in the bay window of the dining room. I was facing the waves as they ran up the beach, but all I could see was Mrs. Holman's car. She would be getting out of Cambridge by now, fighting the traffic. I fixed my mind and hopes on her car. I imagined it pulling up into the driveway and hearing her moan from behind the steering wheel as she sensed the intrusion. I might have told her what we had done, but it wouldn't be real to her until she saw the house.

The house would not appear to be that different, but it was. It would no longer be just hers. I kept on seeing that car, waiting for it to come. As I sat drinking coffee, I envisioned that Mrs. Holman's car would pull into the driveway slowly, feebly and without the confidence of an expensive, upper-class car. A nice car might make me feel justified for living off of the serenity of this home. That scared me. I hoped that Mrs. Holman's car would be dented, faded, somehow slightly battered and used so that it might better fit my image of what the victim must look like.

Germinating

for Taylor Lynne

*T*here was that time, that series of years, fifteen through seventeen, that passed in such a manner that it felt like one long, evolutionary drag of a time-ignorant year. I had been lucky then, or so I thought, through the time of thirteen and fourteen. Puberty had been kind. Not many pimples, no cracked voice, no incredibly frog-like legs. It seemed as if the flow of events in my family, the family itself, or the death of what youth lived in it, willed me to be older without much thought or feeling of the passage.

There was no anxiety, no interaction with girls, or should I have called them *women*? I can't remember what my mother called them. Maybe *ladies*? I felt nothing. For or against. To or from. They were just there, my father had me believe, like paintings, like distance, like my mother, or my great aunt, Lauralinda, and her territorial smile.

Nothing very eventful or strikingly different occurred until the year that was seventeen came along. There wasn't a new car to be excited about, or even a driver's license, but sometime during a series of hot, dusty, columbine days in early June there was that family reunion in Denver.

Some memories of my childhood are more vivid than others, either vaulting into or escaping from the white space of daydreams and the ghosts of rules I affirm or deny as having followed, gone against or forgotten. I envision scores and columns of relatives in some of my daydreams, so many of them are now left behind in the trapped time of that reunion; others remain clearly distinct and alive, and a small few flit in and out of my head like standard bearers to the army of my most elusive memories.

What I often remember first is the dust and visible heat of City Park and the weight of mile-high air on some of the older relatives who sat under large oaks, trying to fan themselves free of their breathlessness and discomfort. I remember relatives grouped by common names and similar smiles, but I also remember never noticing so many different shades of brown skin in one place. I remember there being too many people, too large of a mass for me to receive any one part of them to mark with lasting clarity beyond that day. Then I remember that they are my family.

The folks migrated to that park in Denver much the same way they had moved North and West drifting from the Post-Reconstruction, traveling with a sense of promise and unhurried urgency. They came slowly to Denver, as old people do: on trains, not planes, driving reliable Chryslers and Chevys and riding in back seats with pillows and magazines to ease the wear of the long trek.

I was sitting on a concrete bench watching my relatives who were holding paper plates of cold chicken and looking for someone to embrace. My father sat next to me and told me what it was like to be them: old and still outliving the rest from year to year. A whole group, a whole parkful, an entire family, missing somebody to hold. I gave this some thought, but I was also doing my best to look indignant for having been forced to be there. My father's words rolled off me, and soon I was into my chicken, greasing my cheeks.

"Just like every child your age: sit and eat, tend to yourself . . . That better be the best chicken you ever ate, boy." The voice, from behind me, cut into my ears, and I lowered my plate to my lap. I turned around and rose.

"Ohhh, hello, Auntie Lin—I mean, Lauralinda." I hugged her small body. "I was so glad that you decided to come. I didn't think you would."

My great aunt, Lauralinda, who hated to be called Auntie Lin, stiffened slightly in my grasp and then broke free. She tried to appear as if she were looking for something in her purse. Her purse was very large. I thought to myself that it might be funny to ask her if it were meant to carry everything she had brought with her from California. But I looked at the rich, serious tone of her light brown face and knew that she wouldn't laugh.

In the shade of low branches, her posture avoided an easy guess of her age. She showed years, but I couldn't tell how many. My grandmother used to tell me that her sister liked to stand in the shade because it showed off the tone of her light carmel-rich skin without the haze to give it a yellowish appearance.

I stood there wondering what to say. Her face wore an expression that made me feel that she was about to say something, but she just looked at me. I was too young to realize it then, but I think that she had a way of making you speak to her first. A real "lady" would never speak first. I stood there, not knowing that it was meant for me to say something.

"Well, Lin, hah, have you tried the potato salad?" My father started in. "Ole Gail has done it up good again!" He ate while he spoke, alternating food with words and pocketing chunks of potato in his cheeks to enunciate what she craned to hear. "And how 'bout that chicken? Damn!"

I noticed that Aunt Lin had no plate to hold and she wrung her hands. She looked like she didn't want to be holding anything.

My father continued to eat, not paying attention to whether she answered or not.

"Hey Dad," I said, "I need some more Kool-Aid. You going over to the drinks?"

"Noooo sir! Chicken's too damn good! You got young legs, boy, get it yourself!"

We three stood there for a long moment, my father still eating, Aunt Lin and I watching him eat, both of us understanding the situation. She didn't say anything. She looked at my father and he stopped eating. I figured that she must have practiced a long time to get that expression, and it must have been one that I was raised to recognize, because it made me want to leave. Then again, maybe it wasn't really that look, but instead my own uneasiness. I only knew the weight of her stare.

With a quiet voice made audible by the shakiness of it, she leaned to my father and gestured with her hand, "Roland, go get some beer."

And as if a lever had been pulled, my father went off in search of the beer cooler. I watched him walk away, thinking how out of place he looked at this reunion: bright blue seersucker and red bow tie. He always had an appearance of forced change about him that led people to say, *well, my, Roland, you have changed . . . hair cut? lost weight?* Last year it was yellow pants and a green double-knit shirt.

Aunt Lin was looking straight ahead, her hand still half raised in the gesture that had sent my father off. She was looking at something far away in the rippling haze of heat beyond the shade of the oak trees.

"Your father . . ." She reached for something in her purse, "he isn't a bright man. Is he?" Her concern for wrecking whatever conception I had of my father was secondary to whatever was in the leather-looking vinyl bag that she carried like a baby. From her purse she pulled out a large lace handkerchief. The handkerchief was fine, perfect, and yet this moment was uneasy to me. The air, the mass of relatives, my father, Aunt Lin's strange pale-green hat, which I'd just noticed. I only had a feeling that I should say something. We looked funny, both silent, both still standing.

"Yeah . . . I mean, yes, Dad is sorta weird at times." Something better than that.

She caught my eyes before I could look away. "Weird? I didn't say *weird,* child." She flashed the cloth. " 'Not bright' is what I was meaning. *Dim-witted.* Understand?"

"Just s'pose it's that beer, Auntie. With that tie he does look kinda simple, though," I said it quickly and made an attempt for my neglected chicken.

"Son, some people *look* simple and some just *are.*" She seemed satisfied with herself and began to fold the kerchief into a neat triangle. She dabbed the cloth roughly around her lips, unknowingly removing bits of flaking makeup.

"Sit down," she told me.

And we sat. At that age, I had begun to figure out the importance of conversations that I would have with adults by the tone of their voice when they told me to sit. Usually my mother was best at directing me; her powers of implication were phenomenal. It didn't take more than a very simple, quiet, *let's sit for a while.* Or sometimes it was just a look, like in a social setting where she could not rely on my ability to understand her spoken implications; she knew that look would land me. Something about *that* look. It was damn powerful. I can remember my father driving home drunk from an Orioles game explaining to me that it was important for women to have that look. He breathed it out in a half mumble and never explained why, but the thought intrigued me. After my father had set me off on that thinking, I considered myself an expert at tracking that look down. I was certain that my sister had grasped the notion of it by the time she was three, and I figured that my only defense was the ability to recognize it.

I looked at Aunt Lin for a long while. It was different with her; no implications. I remember she once said that *ladies* could be indirect when it was absolutely necessary, but otherwise it was frivolous; ladies who get what they want are direct. She studied the channels of fabric in her handkerchief. Very direct.

"You really shouldn't stare at old people," she said.

"Just noticing your hat." I told her it looked nice.

"Shouldn't lie either."

"Sorry."

"Shouldn't have to apologize all the time."

"Sor—Okay." We sat there for some time. I was watching my Uncle Jimmy from Milwaukee try to explain the rules of horseshoe-throwing to some second cousins when I heard my aunt sigh deeply. It was a breath that sounded more like fatigue than boredom. She took off her hat, set it in her lap, and began to poke at it with the hairpin that had held it there. Amazing. The youth of her hair. Her face. She looked at me with a curve to her mouth, and I thought she must have smiled like that when she was a child.

"It's an ugly hat." She looked to the horseshoe game. "I didn't have to worry about looking my best here. And besides—"

"Isn't that the hat that Ginny gave you?"

She turned to me quickly at the mention of my other great aunt.

"Yes."

Her sister, Ginny, had always been too flashy for Lauralinda's taste. Ginny carried clutches. Lauralinda had a purse. And she only wore a light foundation makeup to highlight her light brown skin. Ginny had proudly brandished red lips throughout her life.

I started to say sorry. While she watched the game, I looked at her hair, knotted up neatly, perfectly. It was too shiny, as if it were not her own. I could not help staring at it; I had never seen her without a hat outside of her house. All these years, hidden under hats and in the dim light of her home in San Diego, her hair had not aged. Barely any color was gone.

At that time, when privacy and mystery were everything to a boy my age, it seemed to me that the deep brown on her head was her best kept secret. I felt deeply satisfied in that.

"I wonder where your father has got off to." She began working to put her hat back on. She was just filling dead space, a true lady holding up her part of a conversation; I felt that she didn't really want an answer. I didn't want to reply.

She was still struggling with the hairpin. All I could do was watch her. *Shouldn't stare at old folks.* I reached to help, but she pulled away and quickly jabbed the pin into the hat on her head so that it stuck at an odd angle, like an antenna. I wanted to laugh. It was obvious that it was not as perfect as she would have wanted, but she had done it herself, without help. She didn't need to look for the mirror in her purse.

Across from us, the horseshoe folks had taken a break to grab a new batch of ribs off the grill. Someone yelled about getting some more pictures. Someone else hooted about getting more beer. They were good folks. They wore their best leisure clothes. Hugged each other. They laughed with their teeth showing.

Aunt Lin still faced the horseshoe poles. Her hands rubbed her thighs.

"You don't understand what's going on here, do you, child?" She watched the wind sweep the grass. She just sat there, waiting for me.

"Well, I don't know. There's a lot of people here I've never seen. I don't know them."

She sighed and clutched her purse.

"Good. That's . . . . . . good." She turned to me and her face looked weakened. I thought she might cry, but she put the handkerchief to use and covered her face; somehow it prevented tears.

"That's very good in a way," she breathed. "It's really not worth it. You're too young to know it, but these folks really don't matter. It seems like you can hug them all now, get to know them for a few days, but soon they'll leave. They'll be gone."

"Well, we can't always be together, Auntie," I laughed. "That'd have to be an awful big house if—"

"No." There was a slight wheeze in her voice, but then strength. "No. They will leave you."

"Auntie?"

"This is the last one of these damn things I'm coming to. It's not worth it. Spent a whole life getting away from these crazy people. And now you come back and they don't understand what's going on. Trifling Negroes. They're worthless. They just leave you. And it doesn't even matter; they never had any class anyhow." There was sweat at her temples, and she looked off towards some of the older relatives sitting near the drink table. "Soon they'll all be gone. Take your pictures now; only way they'll ever look like *somebody*."

For a moment I lost the sense of where I was. All of those relatives seemed to be floating through the park, blending into and separating from one another, and the visions of those who were dead lurched out of a past that my parents had pressed on me. I could envision the mass of my family at some point dispersing and slipping from me as I grew older, carried away on silent waves. I imagined myself on some expanse of water, watching them drift to different bodies of land. There was Aunt Lin, sitting on a beach at sunrise, much like the beaches my grandmother had told me about, where they used to go as girls and look for sea shells. I envisioned Aunt Lin sitting on that beach holding her arms to her body as if their frailty might make them fall off. She had her face held high, not smiling, but also not frowning, not appearing to want much of anything more than what she had right then. She was looking into the sun. She was the only one on that beach.

"I don't like pictures all that much, Auntie," I said, feeling a need to breathe.

"Well you better start!" She seemed surprised at me, and I couldn't meet her gaze. Her voice came out clear and definite. "You'll come to care about them. You have to. You won't even want to; you'll reject them, but you can't get away from them."

I was hearing her, but I was also forming and editing a picture in my head of my mother, father, sister and me as the only passengers on some cruise ship just off the shore of the daydream beach where my aunt was. I wasn't sure where we were going. It felt like a long way away, though. And I couldn't swim.

"You don't like your mother, do you?"

"No, I do . . . I—"

"Or your father. It's all right. I figured you were lonely; that's why I came over. Not good to hate so much and be so lonely. Not yet, child."

We sat and stared at parallel horizons, each with our own focal point, but both out past the shade of the trees, the overflowing trashcans, the sand boxes of the horseshoe pits and even further, beyond even the near flawless green of the golf course. If we had been on a pier, we might have been looking at the same harbor entrance for different boats to arrive.

"You don't like *me* much, do you?" She didn't look at me.

"I—I don't know, Auntie."

"You better not. You're better off that way." She gave out another life-tired sigh. "Besides, you kids these days don't know how to treat a lady. Stare too much." And then she giggled like she had let out another secret.

I looked over to where most of the relatives were lining up to get ribs. I barely knew any of them. One man, my third cousin Clifford, was trying to take pictures, but he was standing against the sun, and the relatives were reluctant to get their photos taken. Finally, he took a few poor shots to satisfy himself that he could take them whenever he wanted, and put his camera down. I had the feeling that Aunt Lin was watching me watch cousin Clifford. I turned and met her eyes looking at me. Many things hit my head right then: the quality of anger that lies hidden between the known and the unknown, people who were cared for dearly, too much, not enough. Relatives lost and found. Drifting and forgotten. Alone.

And the thought of my aunt's hair, unraveled, in the dark, far away in San Diego, spread on some clean sheet for no one to see, not my grandmother nor even her other sister, Ginny, now dead. And the photographs that would come from this strange family reunion. Remembrances through eyes such as Clifford's. We looked at each other a long time, my Aunt Lauralinda and I. Shouldn't stare at old folks. I smiled. I tried to imagine the picture that we might make together.

"That really *is* a nice hat you've got, Auntie."

She eyed me, looking as if she meant to break the confidence of my compliment. I thought she might tell me to leave. But then her face softened, a hint of that young girl's secret smile.

She looked away for a moment and then back. Her fingers were working the leather straps of her purse in the absence of something to hold. Maybe we both felt like hugging each other right then.

I got up slowly, not worrying about saying "sorry." I went off to get Aunt Lauralinda a plate of chicken, thinking how when I got back I would ask her about hunting for sea shells on the beach at sunrise, and she would take all afternoon to tell me. I would listen quietly, not bored nor bitter, sitting there with her, smiling.

About the Author

William Henry Lewis was born in Denver, Colorado
in 1967, and grew up in Seattle, Washington, D.C., and
Chattanooga. He graduated from Trinity College in 1989 and
received a Master of Fine Arts degree from the University
of Virginia in 1994. He has devoted himself to a wide range
of activities, including performance art, coaching lacrosse
and counseling people in low-income communities. His
play, "Peeling Potatoes," was produced at Trinity College
and several other locations. In 1993 and 1994, respectively,
"The Days the Light Stays On" and "Other People's Houses"
were awarded the University of Virginia's Balch Prize
for the best story by a graduate student. Lewis is an assis-
tant professor teaching creative writing and literature at
Denison University.